About the Author

Jonny Carr had always been inspired by mythology and the idea of heroes. During his life he had wanted to create a story about a lone hero pitted against the world. Studying media at Seaford College and earning a distinction star inspired him to create his own myth, ultimately culminating in *The Godslayer.*

The Godslayer

Jonny Carr

The Godslayer

Olympia Publishers
London

www.olympiapublishers.com
OLYMPIA PAPERBACK EDITION

A CIP catalogue record for this title is
available from the British Library.

ISBN: 978-1-80439-183-9

First Published in 2023

Olympia Publishers
Tallis House
2 Tallis Street
London
EC4Y 0AB

Printed in Great Britain

Dedication

I dedicate this to my friends, family and my teachers who believed in me from the start.

Acknowledgements

Thank you to my friends, Izzy, Nelson, Harry, Dan and Evie for the encouragement, support and always believing in me. A huge acknowledgement to the staff of Shamley Green Stores for giving me a chance.

Chapter 1

The Great Beginning

Let me tell you a tale. About the greatest story ever told, woven like a stitch into the fabric of time itself. A tale of heroes and villains. Good and evil. Gods and monsters.

Once before time, there were eight giant humanoid beings made of pure starlight. They are what was, before there was anything. The primes. The first to be called Gods. Deities amongst nothing. Each represented a primal core consisting of a unique trait and personality;

Akush — Strength and honour
Voraxni — Dreams and wonder
Melok — Mind and intelligence
Benatar — Despair and grief
Xyr — Knowledge and sharing
Dune — Connection and family
Nera — Love and joy
Thanashade — Death and emotion

These beings were at constant strife with one another. A war that echoed across the infinite blackness of nothing. Each blow ripping the fabric of space and time. Tearing it apart. But also forging it too. It wasn't until Akush, the prime of strength, struck his brother Thanashade, the prime of death, that a bang occurred. The shockwave ripped the primes apart, sending their bodies of light into the infinite everything. Thus came the universe and the first stars.

Being highly omnipotent as they are, they cannot be so easily quelled by a meagre bang. Their bodies refabricated and reformed themselves with new bright light, and they watched.

Their creation laid bare before them. They felt no rage, hate or anger towards one another any more. Only responsibility to the lights. Their war led to the stars, the first children of the universe, and they had to parent it.

They learnt to tame the solar winds, carve the foundation of galaxies and nurture the elements of change and evolution. They created the first lifeform on a desolate planet.

They named him Goron, who had the appearance of a giant silver bipedal gorilla. The primes watched with glee and merry thought as he took his first steps.

They nurtured him as he grew and grew from the size of a mountain to a star. Akush taught him the value of strength.

Voraxni, the power of dreams and ideas.

Melok, the wisdom of the mind.

Benatar, the danger of despair.

Xyr, the value of knowledge.

Dune, the importance of connection.

Nera, the joys of love.

Thanashade, the impermanence of life, leading to death.

They made him a God.

However, the primes' life began to wane. Spreading their power over the universe for over a thousand millenniums began to take its toll on their spirits. They were dying. It would soon be up to Goron to shepherd the cosmos. Sensing their demise, the primes bestowed upon Goron a final gift. Their combined powers. They gathered in a circle around their son. Goron looked upon them for guidance and reassurance. The primes' starlight bodies began to disassemble, and levitated towards Goron. The bright lights were absorbed into Goron's body. The overwhelming power made him mad with pain, but he soon came back to his senses. His eyes now glowing blue with omnipotence. His new senses and perception of time and reality made everything seem small and minute. He was no longer a God. He was God.

Goron decided to venture to a small planet near the centre of existence. There was something about it that drew him there. He shrank himself to a more practical size as he entered its field of gravity. When he touched the surface, it was barren with nothing but rock and dust, but Goron felt something was here. He knelt down. Placed his palm on the surface and closed his eyes. Breathed in… and out. Breathed in… and out. There! He found what drew him here. Fire. The raging fire within this planet was strong. Too strong to ignore. It wanted to be unleashed. To be free. Alive. Goron opened his eyes and stood upright. With a flick of his wrist, a mighty axe appeared before him and he grasped it so, raising it above his head. Widened his stance. He gave a mighty roar and thrust the axe down with all his godly might into the bedrock. Fire and lava erupted with a force hitherto undreamt of, and the ground shook and screamed. The whole surface was soon enveloped in fire. Goron stood mighty and unharmed and whispered…

"Earth."

Goron continued to develop his 'Earth' for many millennia. He carved the oceans, chiselled the mountains and planted the jungles. He soon turned his attention to recreating the phenomena that led to him. Creating life. To do this, he grabbed a huge boulder, but in his hands it looked no bigger than a small pebble. He brought it closer to his mouth and breathed on it, his life force pouring into the stone, enhancing it with his power. He then buried it in the middle of a desert, and soon a mighty great tree grew, eventually to heights greater than himself. The bark was faultless; the leaves were radiant. From a branch, grew a seed. Goron plucked it and the cocoon soon cracked and split open. Inside, the first human.

Not long after, many humans were birthed from the great tree; and on the other branches, all manner of creatures were concocted. Horse, cattle, fish, birds and many others. The ecosystem was flourishing and humanity flourished, building the first civilisation, worshipping their God, holding many celebrations and feasts in his honour. He vowed to protect them from all cosmic threats.

However, all was not well. For unbeknownst to even Goron, there was another celestial being, waiting, watching and lurking in the blackness of the cosmos. His antithesis. A reflection of Goron's light. A dark shadow. The Dark God.

No one knows from where or whence this malevolent shadow originated, but it had found Goron. It had found life.

The Dark God had the appearance of a black dragon. Its wings brought solar hurricanes and were wide enough to blacken any sun. Its tail could wrap around an entire ocean. His claws could pierce through godflesh. Its fire, rife with rot and decay.

This avatar of the dark flew to Earth, Goron soon felt its presence approaching. He rushed across continents to meet this force, until he came to stand before the life tree.

The Dark God was waiting. Perched along one of the branches, like an owl. The bark had twisted, deformed as if sickened by its touch. The leaves had withered and died. Its eyes, an unapproachable, unfriendly yellow.

"What are you?" Goron spoke with thunderous defence in a tongue no one could replicate or speak from.

The creature just watched. Silent. Goron flicked his wrist and a gleaming silver sword appeared. He gripped with two hands. The creature stayed silent. Along the branch where the creature was perched, a seed fell to the ground. It was bigger than usual, uglier too, green with purple veins. It cracked and split, and inside… A dinosaur. A carnivorous beast. An abomination. In Goron's eyes, it was akin to blasphemy.

The Dark God had used the tree to create life in its own image, its own worshippers, its own cult. It bore his fangs and bit into the trunk. Soon, the whole tree twisted and screamed with change. The leaves fell. The wood splintered. All the seeds fell. Broken. Replaced by the dark spawn of the dragon.

Goron howled and the dragon reciprocated a scream back at him, baring tooth and claw. Each rushed toward one another. The great battle had begun, a true clash of titans. Goron spun his sword back and forth, cleaving scale and flesh when he could land a hit. The dragon did not flinch. Instead it whipped its tail, striking Goron in the chest sending him flying across continents. He landed with a thud into a snow scraped mountain that shook the Earth. He was hurt, with his chest pumping purple blood out. A shadow fell upon him blocking the sun, but he knew it was no shadow. The dragon breathed what looked like thick smoke from its agape jaws. Goron hastily stood and ran. The smoke poisoned whatever it touched, killing and rotting everything, turning the land into a twisted nightmare.

Goron slid down the snow as fast as he could, he had lost his sword during the flight. A new plan was needed. He looked behind to find the screaming beast right behind him. It grabbed him and bit into his shoulder, making him lose balance and cry in pain. They rolled down, ungracefully, punching and roaring at one another.

They flew off of cliffs, ridges and peaks, until finally stopping at the base of the mountain. They broke apart. Each glaring at the other. The war was far from done.

The story had only just begun.

Their strife would continue for another hundred million years, but in their eyes it was mere hours. Dinosaurs ruled the Earth, Man was all but wiped out. Only a few tribes remained, hidden in the shadows with fear.

The Dark God had nearly won his prize, the only thing left was his foe. This whole endeavour, however, distracted Goron from his vow of defending Earth, as, unbeknownst to him, a meteor was headed straight for it. The bright luminescence of the meteor overflowed the sky with red and orange. The titans ceased their fight, and gazed at the sky. Goron howled in anguish and sadness, he came to his senses that time had flowed much faster than he perceived whilst he was caught in the ecstasy of war. His creations were nearly extinct. The dragon meanwhile showed its first emotion. Laughter. A kind of laugh that even the deaf would hear and shrivel at. The light grew brighter and the rumbling came. Closer, and closer. Goron shut his eyes, awaiting the inevitable.

A flash. A bang. Fire. Death. Silence.

Goron coughed himself awake. His once radiant coat of fur was now tarnished with soot and ash. His wounds had been cauterised by the fires thankfully, he was no longer bleeding. He stood and looked at his surroundings. He had been asleep for a while. A few thousand years maybe. It was surreal to him that the land looked almost the same as it had once done all those years ago before he helped unleash the Earth. All that time and effort, reduced to rubble. He grieved.

But his grief was not to last as he soon found himself attacked by the dragon once more and pinned to the ground. It was still laughing. But Goron knew what he must do. His last resort. A desperate and desolate plan.

He clenched his fist and hit the ground, splitting and cracking it wide open. The two titans fell into the chasm. And fall they did. All the way to the Earth's core. Goron ripped the dragon's wings, breaking them as they fell closer to the sphere of fire that was the planet's beating core. Goron gripped onto a protruding rock harshly and suddenly, stopping his fall. The dragon continued to plummet to its fiery grave. And burn. But still, it laughed. Goron could not help but watch his foe burn with satisfaction.

The core however could not handle this dark energy, and its light. Its life. Was snuffed out. The spark was extinguished. The Earth was dead.

Goron recovered the dragon's body. He climbed out of the giant chasm. The scenery was dead. Even the grey looked bleaker.

Although the dragon was dead. Its power lingered still. To prevent any other celestial who may be out there from using its great power, he crafted a tomb inside a pocket universe. A labyrinth of mazes, traps and dark sorcery to keep everything and anything out, and placed the body in a great sarcophagus. The Tomb of the Dark God.

To prevent any entry further still, the entrance to this dark dimension was split into seven pieces. These pieces took forms of their own over time.

A terrifying monster the size of a mountain.

An obsidian box, filled with evil, despair and malicious intent.

A fading heart, that continuously breaks, whilst searching for a body to finally rest in.

A spear of the finest craftsmanship, that grants great power to the wielder.

A pair of eyes, revealing scorching truths that would otherwise remain hidden.

A bow made of crystallised lightning.

Finally, a blue serpent, that will grow to encompass the world.

With the tomb complete, there was one job left. He would sacrifice his heart to reboot the earth. He ventured back to the lifeless core. Ripped open his chest and a stream of light left his body and into the core. Light began to flicker and soon, it shone brighter than it had ever done before. All life that had ever lived on Earth would be brought back, except the wicked creations the dragon birthed.

Goron's body fell. He was dead. But his death carved the way for the great pantheons. His power lived on and took the forms of new Avatars, like Zeus, Odin, Indra, Osiris and more. These new beings gravitated to the surface which was now green with life. They saw the humans, who were afraid. The Gods reached out their hands and the humans accepted.

But more power was unleashed. Avatars of chaos like the Titans and demons. Goron's dark hatred lived on too. The hatred of himself and others like his kind. The hatred and power of the Godslayer. My gift. My curse.

Chapter 2

The Cycle Begins Anew

"DANTE!" The sinister voice wakes me again, screaming my name like a monstrous amalgamation of various voices. I needed to stop watching horror movies late at night. I knew that. They kept me awake more often than not. But what better time for scares and frights than when Halloween is right around the corner.

Today is October 29th. Today, would be a day to remember.

I've been married for two years to my wonderful wife Mrs Mia Adler (Nee Torrance). We met at school. I was bullied frequently because of my weird hair colour. A hybrid of somewhere between dark red and purple. But when she and her stepbrother Marcus Pryer came, they didn't see a freak. They saw someone who needed people who had his back. And they obliged to fill this position. Marcus was a beefy lad, but a bit shorter than average, who liked the gym almost as much as he did his looks. His father was a firefighter who lost his life when Marcus was a baby. His mother married Mia's father after her mother had left them for a wealthy Italian man.

Now that we are all in our late twenties, we are officially grown-ups. Marcus joined the army, worked his way to the SAS, and is currently on tour. Mia writes books. Her most famous work is Wolf Kissed. A story about a young girl who falls in love with a werewolf. It's also now a major Hollywood film series. I meanwhile am a stuntman, mainly working on motorbikes and wirework, but I want to do some proper acting. In fact, I have a part in the upcoming Angry Speed Eight as the henchman, Snake.

But today is all about love. I started to get feelings for her when I was sixteen. As she was beautiful and because of how the social hierarchy seems to work in school, she was in the 'popular' group. I was still being called names like 'flame head' by that time still. It was almost smart. I was a nerd, I loved pop culture and entertainment. But she treated me good still, and with respect. I asked her out, she gave me a shot and the rest is history. Marcus was even my best man. Came back from tour especially for the wedding.

I think I saw Larry (One of the mean populars) working as a garbage man once. Gotta love Karma.

I showered in the en suite, cleaned up, made myself look sexy and nice, got dressed, put on my nice black Star Wars themed shirt, black trousers and got my leather jacket ready for later.

Wait, I forgot, my medication. I open the bedside table and pull out a can of prescribed tablets. A type called omnitoxike. Stuff you wouldn't find in most pharmacies. It's legal, but you need special prescription from a Doctor. They are to help with my ongoing migraines I've had since I was a child. I swear sometimes it felt like there's a voice in my head shouting at me in what feels like all capitals. Weird right?

Tablets in mouth, a sip of water and done, now to see Mia downstairs.

We lived in a nice house in Guildford, Surrey, where we grew up. Our families were close by which was nice. Downstairs, the décor was very modern and sleek, white and black colours, with pictures and frames hung up of things like fields and meadows, but not too pretentious with showing off our lifestyle. Mia was in the living room.

"Hello beautiful." she says to me. Sitting on our leather sofa.

"Shouldn't I say that to you? I thought men were dubbed handsome?"

"No, not quite." She gets up from the sofa, walks towards me and wraps her hands around my head "You haven't shown me how manly you are yet" she continues.

"Then let me show you." We kiss. A loving, sweet and caring kiss.

A thought crosses my mind.

"Let's go get breakfast." I start.

"Well breakfast is conveniently placed in the kitchen."

"No I mean out. At a café."

She pauses. "Who are you and what have you done with my 'never do anything new or spontaneous' husband."

"I killed him and took his place. Obviously." We share a laugh. "No I just feel like we should go out, The Fox maybe."

"Okay. Let me get my coat." She detaches from me and walks to the hall but I still feel her warmth. "Your idea, you're paying," she continues.

I follow to the hallway, where she is putting on her white fluffy coat, it's still fresh outside and there is a little bit of snow, but it should warm up by later in the day. I grab my black coat and put my hood up.

"Oh darling, I hope you're putting that up to keep your ears warm and not to hide your hair."

I pause. "No." She is right though, as much as I claim otherwise. I still feel a bit self-conscious about my hair. Some days I am more confident than others. I have tried to dye it, but it never works.

She gives me a look like she doesn't believe me, but doesn't bring the subject back up again. We leave the house.

The Fox is about a ten-minute walk from our house. We chat along the way, hand in hand, about how her friend's sister's nephew's wife is, 'like, so having an affair', in her words. And about other important topics like parties and nightclubs. I had never been so intrigued in my life (Not). She then brought up children…

"Margaret's having a baby."

"Who?"

"My friend."

"The one whose sister's nephew's wife is having an affair?" She hits me playfully.

"No. She's the one who smokes."

"A lot of people you know smoke."

She pauses.

"The one who stuck a cucumber up her… You know."

It goes off like a lightbulb strapped to fireworks in my head.

"Oh Margaret Hastings, how could I forget someone like that?"

We both share an awkward silence after this. Children is an awkward subject for either one of us to bring up. We haven't really talked about having kids, but the silence says it's on both of our minds, overthinking about what the other's opinion is. But no more on the topic was said for the trip.

Inside, the café was decorated with orange and brown, probably to simulate the outdoorsy nature of its name, but it was welcoming, quaint and familiar.

We walk in, but as we are, a big hulking man in a long trench coat, with long blonde hair, walks into me…

I see a white blinding flash in my head. I see the man covered in blood, naked. Screaming and cursing the Gods of Olympus. I see him ripping off a giant lion's head, and he begins to drink its blood. I hear a name.

Herakles.

Another flash, and the visions are gone. The man is looking straight at me. With hate.

"You…" he says coldly.

I say nothing and walk in. The man was still watching me from the outside through the glass window panels. It's strange. I think I knew him, and hated him.

After our meals (I had scrambled eggs on toast and Mia had a hard-boiled egg) we began the trek home. The man had left, to where I don't know. But I still felt he wasn't far.

"Who was that guy?" Mia questioned as she opened the front door.

"I don't know."

"Did you know him?"

"No. Didn't recognise him." (Lie. I vaguely did, strangely enough).

We took our jackets off, then retreated into the living room. She leant into me on the sofa. It was just like a romantic movie. We put the TV on and watched old episodes of *Top Gear*. One of our favourites. Not so much the new ones with the new presenters.

My mind was elsewhere though. Those images of that man. I could still feel his emotions, rage and sadness. But were those images true? Or did I imagine them? I did watch a horror the night before. But this felt real to me.

It was now 3.50 p.m. We hastily started to get ready, as we were off to London, meeting our friends Clyde and Regina Zellar for the night, getting drunk and going to nightclubs. Clyde and Regina were both models and got invites to the premiere of a new nightclub called Devil's Little Sinners, owned by eccentric millionaire Bob Chase. They invited us along as we were the 'best looking' of our friends so would fit in better. I put on a thin layered hoodie before my leather jacket. It was still a bit cold. Colder than was forecasted. I waited downstairs by the door. I heard footsteps from the top floor and there she was… Mia was dressed in white, a pure colour. The polar opposite to my completely black attire. She gracefully walked down the stairs like a Disney princess. Everything slowed down. I was star struck.

"You look beautiful," I said like a nervous schoolboy talking to his crush.

"And you look handsome."

We smiled and kissed.

The train station was too far to walk. So I suggested we go in style. In the garage I had a Ducati motorbike, which I inherited from my father when he died. I loved my bike. To feel the wind be brushed aside as I raced along was equal to no other type of ecstasy.

My dad, Joseph Adler, was a complicated man. We had our ups and downs. He pushed me to always be on top. But he didn't, couldn't or wouldn't understand my anxieties, struggles or mental state. My mum, Amy Adler, was always kinder.

I sometimes felt that Joseph loved his bike more than me, watching him work and tinker on it like a grease monkey almost every day. Sometimes he'd let me help. He died after he got too drunk one evening and fell off a bridge and into a river. I feel like this bike was his last gift to me and it's my responsibility to keep it going and working, because if I don't, his ghost will be disappointed in me.

It took some persuasion to get Mia on the bike. She did like the bike, but didn't like to go too fast, especially as she had just had her hair done. Thankfully, we were blessed by the miraculous invention of helmets, which we were lucky enough to own.

We sat on the seats, Mia's arms wrapped around my chest. I put the key in the ignition. Turned and felt the bike purr and roar into life.

A short trip later, and we've arrived. Guildford Train Station. There were all kinds of people gathering up with their friends at the station. There were Chavs, Stag parties, Goths and more making their appearance. I parked the bike whilst Mia got the tickets.

Inside, the crowds were hustling. Gathering last minute snacks from M&S or returning from work. The schedule board hung up said that a train was coming to platform four in two minutes. The next one, not for another hour.

"Must be why it's so busy," I said.

"Quickly!" she replied.

We begin to do a fast, walking pace bordering on a slight jog, Mia is ahead of me, when suddenly a word races across my mind like lightning on speed. Imprinting itself into my brain like a cheap tattoo.

"WALLET."

I stop in my tracks. Feeling a little like whiplash.

"Mia," I shouted, "I forgot my wallet."

She stops ahead in her stride and looks back at me, with an

upset and angry face.

"What? How could you forget your wallet when going up to London?" She shouts back. We share a silence between us, drowning out the moving populace around us. I start…

"Go on without me. I'll get the next train. I'll meet you at the club."

"What? You sure?"

"Yeah, you wouldn't want to go on the bike again at hyper speed now, would you?"

"No, Fair point, see you soon darling." She blows a kiss to me and resumes the journey to the platform.

I could hear the crowds shoving to get on the train as I paced to the bike, followed swiftly by silence from the station. I put my hands in my jacket pocket, then it strikes me. I feel an object in my grasp. I pull it out. My wallet.

I was not in a good mode, whilst sitting on a bench waiting for the train. The atmosphere was still and silent. I couldn't hear any form of life. I didn't even notice that I was the only one in the station until I dropped my phone. No trains. No announcements. No people. I felt like Harry Potter before the Night Bus picked him up in the third movie. When he was being hunted…

"DUCK," a voice which sounded like it was in all capitals came to me.

Without a microsecond of judgement or hesitation, I lunged forward onto my stomach. I saw overhead something was thrown at me. Something that no man could throw. I lifted my head off the ground and looked forward. I was struck by fear. My bike. It was destroyed before me. Someone, just tried to kill me… by throwing a bike. My Bike!

"Found you."

I recognised the voice. The man from earlier. I heard a loud thud and a creeping crack behind. I slowly turned and saw him…

He was dressed like He-Man, gauntlets, boots and pants made of gold and fur. He had an image of an eagle branded into his chest. His skin was slightly golden. He looked even bigger than before. Eight feet perhaps. With muscles that should not be biologically possible. He carried with him a giant sword. Too giant that anyone could wield and held it in one hand like it were a freshly snapped twig! He sheathes it after eyeing me up and down. Thinking I'm not worth dulling the blade with a hit from my body. The voice in my head came back with a name…

"HERAKLES," it said.

Chapter 3

The Thirteenth Labour

"Killing you, will finally grant me entry to the White City," the hulking man boasted.

I was still rife with confusion and paranoia. I could only think to ask one thing…

"Who are you?" I asked.

"I TOLD YOU, THAT IS HERAKLES."

There it is again, that voice in my head, rattling like a snake in the scorching desert.

"I am Herakles, son of Zeus, slayer of the Nemean Lion and tamer of Cerberus," he continued to boast. I think he likes the sound of his own voice. I couldn't think of what to say or do. My legs are frozen with fear but still feel like jelly. I finally muster what little courage I have…

"I thought Hercules was the son of Zeus."

My comment wipes the smirk off his face. I can't believe I said that. I've pissed him off even more now.

"Hercules? Fucking Hercules?!" He shouts, losing his cool swaggering tone from before. "How dare you! Do you know nothing? Is that it? What, because you saw some movie where they name me Hercules and you don't bother to question it at all? It's not even a Greek name! You people are so mindless these days!"

He had really lost his cool. I catch him muttering something under his breath…

"Fucking Romans. Mishearing my name. I'm glad I ate them all."

I begin to sneak away as he blows off steam. But Herakles notices and walks in front of me. Every step he makes cracks the ground as if it can't support his immense weight. He points his sword at me.

"You're not going anywhere."

He grabs me with his gargantuan hand around my throat and lifts me to meet his eye line.

"Please, let me go," I squeeze out of my mouth like a broken whistle.

"Your death will finally give me clemency and I can join my family. Think of it as my thirteenth and final labour."

'This is it,' I think to myself. So much happening in so little time. It's not fair. Won't anyone help me?

"YES. I'LL HELP."

Suddenly, my arms reach forward as if on autopilot, without my control, and my hands clasp around his face. My thumbs dig into his eyes. Blood leaks out with a howl of pain from the big man to pair with it. He lets go of me. I fall to the ground on my back, gasping for breath. Herakles has his hands over his face, blood still oozing between his fingers. I begin to crawl away.

"NO."

I freeze. I can't move my body.

"FINISH THIS."

The voice. What is going on? Is it commanding me? Is this real? Is anything real anymore? All these questions, with no rhyme or reason for the events in front of me.

Herakles wipes his eyes, he has healed. He looks down at me with such disgust and hate it sends shivers down my spine like cold wind and water. He grabs my leg and thrusts me into the air. I'm flying, or at least that's what it feels like. The G force echoes and ripples around me like echoes. I finally land with a thud. I'm on a road, but can't tell, where. I hear cars screeching to a halt and hitting one another in the process. I stand, and get my bearings. I recognise this. It's the part of the A3 road that passes through the town. More precisely, the bridge that hangs over a junction below.

"BEHIND YOU!"

But it's too late. I'm hit by a truck that was going way too fast. It hits me off the bridge and into the traffic below. I land on a car windshield. I hear the screaming family inside. The driver puts their foot on the brake and screeches to a halt in an emergency stop and I fly off, rolling into the tarmac. I've never taken a beating like this. God, no one has. I hear Herakles' signature footsteps again. *Crack. Crack.* He has found me.

"Now that was fun to watch!" He jokes.

I can't move. I think I'm paralysed. All my bones are broken. I hope I'm dead. I don't want to live any more. This is too much. It's not fair. I think I'm crying.

"Are you crying? Fucking Pathetic."

Well that settles that debate.

He wraps his tree trunk like fingers around my head and begins to squeeze.

"I want to see the life fade from your eyes. The insides of your head. And I can't wait to drink your brains like chicken soup."

Oh my God. I'm going to die like Oberyn Martell *in Game of Thrones*. I can feel life being denied to me. Air failing to fill my lungs. Just let it be quick. Please.

I scream.

"ENOUGH, I WILL FINISH THIS MYSELF."

Just like that, my body is back on autopilot, my legs flip and wrap around the giant's head like a chokehold, and spin, flipping him off his feet in a quick sweeping movement. He loosens his grip and I escape. This doesn't stop Herakles for long as he quickly regains his footing after his tumble and begins to charge once more, sword unsheathed from his back. Rage racing. Anger churning. He swipes up and down, left and right, but fails to hit me. What is going on? How am I dodging this with no fault? He is getting agitated by his lack of success. His warrior spirit denied a victory. He raises the sword aloft and plummets down like a meteor, but still misses.

He swung his strike so ferociously that the blade is stuck in the ground. My body seems to realise this and swings around and kicks upright into his chin. Uppercut!

The act sends him flying skyward. Crash! He lands into a pile of abandoned cars. Boom, explosions follow suit.

"TAKE THAT YA LITTLE BITCH!" The voice shouts at the top of its non-existent lungs.

A singular tooth hits the tarmac with a little ping and spins like a record. I must have hit him pretty hard.

Herakles rises from the flames, unburnt, like a messiah from a church book. His facial expressions show he is angrier than ever. I can feel the air bubbling and boiling, and not just from the burning cars, but from him and his frustration and humiliation.

I hear an engine coming. A large one. Seven cylinders.

I look to my left and see a large Shell branded oil tanker truck coming towards us and trying to slow down to avoid the carnage. Herakles jumps towards the vehicle and grabs it by its front wheels. He lifts upward. It now looked like a mini skyscraper from New York as it swung aloft. Herakles was holding it like a sports bat.

He swings down his 'bat' at me, causing destruction and mayhem, car parts flying everywhere like an exploding volcano. My body dodges for me. The oil inside was starting to leak like a punctured water bag. I feel something in my hand. It's the sword! I must have been able to pull it out before dodging. Wait… I feel the boiling air again…

Herakles throws a punch towards me from behind, but I duck and slash across his stomach. He tumbles like a lubricated boulder into the tanker and I watch the horror in front of me…

It seems I cut through his stomach lining and intestines, they were spilling out like wet tomato sauce covered spaghetti. A mixture of blood and black goo were overflowing the road. His lunch from earlier spills out. An amalgamation of malformed bodies flows out onto the ground, including what looks like a small child. As well as some still undigested squirrels, rats and fish amongst the gore, offal and other fleshy liquids.

I don't need an autopilot to do what I must. I fling the sword like a boomerang at the spilling oil. The friction of contact ignites sparks and… Kaboom! Fiery inferno engulfs the son of Zeus. His howls drowned out by the fires of defeat.

"FATALITY."

Damn right, strange voice.

"Fatality," I speak back.

Chapter 4

The Blade's History

The sounds of sirens were wallowing nearby. Getting closer and closer to the scene of what is most undoubtedly numerous crimes and violations against breaking the peace.

I begin my exit or escape… (whatever you want to call it).

"WAIT, LOOK BY YOUR FEET."

As if the voice is now my commander, I follow its orders, and sure enough, there is an item of most interest. A shard of Herakles' sword.

"PICK IT UP," it commands.

I follow like a good soldier, and place the sharp object in my jacket pocket. It's still hot like a chip that's just come out of the oven.

"GOOD, NOW HEAD BACK TO THE STATION. THE NIGHT IS STILL YOUNG."

"Wait, I'm not sure what you are, but we just had a fight with a thing, that can only be described as 'The Hulk', you're giving me commands and I'm following. It's all crazy. Besides we don't even know if it's dead!"

The thought doesn't even cross my mind how hysterical and silly I look. To anyone who would be watching, it would look as if I'm having an argument with myself. Which to be frank I'm not even sure if I'm not.

"HE IS MOST UNDOUBTEDLY STILL ALIVE. IT

TAKES MORE THAN THAT TO KILL A DEMI GOD."

I take one last glance into the fires. I see no body.

"He's not dead," I say out loud.

"NO."

"He'll come back?"

"YES."

Arriving at the station was somewhat surreal, like an out of body experience. The crowds had reappeared, as if they never vanished in the first place. Why was it so empty before Herakles arrived? Did he use some sort of magic or sorcery? Was it someone else? And if so, are they still watching me? Thankfully though, the trains were still running, despite the terrorism that occurred across town. I board the train and finally am on the way to London, after a long and very crazy delay.

I quickly make haste to the on-board toilet to check my wounds. Double check to make sure the lock is locked. In the mirror, I see no cuts or bruises, bleeding or broken things. It looks as if I was never in a fight. Except for a few tears on my clothes, I look practically normal. It wasn't thirty minutes ago, I thought I was paralysed. There is one jarring detail I noted however. My eyes look a shade different. I once had blue eyes, but now look like they've turned a shade greener.

I collapse onto the toilet seat, head in hands, looking like I just received some terrible grim news. I'm jolted out of the seat by a familiar voice…

"ROUGH NIGHT, HUH?"

"Oh God, will you just stop!"

"NAH, I STILL HAVE A JOB TO DO, AND MORE IMPORTANTLY, SO DO YOU."

"Who or what exactly are you? And why are you interfering

in my life?"

"LATER, BUT FIRST WE MUST MAKE A STRATEGIC RETREAT TO A FILTHY TRAIN SEAT."

Cut to five minutes later and I'm sitting in a 'filthy' train seat.

"Okay, what now?" I whisper, like I'm in a spy movie.

"TAKE OUT THE SHARD."

I follow swiftly with the instruction. It wasn't as hot any more.

"What now then?"

"ENJOY THE RIDE."

As soon as the voice concludes its phrase, a blinding flash envelops my vision and mind, the exact same way it happened when I first bumped into Herakles.

I see mountains, trees and fields. A beautiful symphony of colours envelops me, like I'm in a storybook. I see a city, but not a modern city, monopolised by towers and money, but a quaint and communal place made of marble and quartz.

The people, they are dressed in tunics or amour. Carrying spears and swords sheathed in scabbards. The soldiers are immortalised with iconic red capes and golden breastplates.

The king of this monolith is named to me.

Leonidas.

I recognise this place now. It's ancient Greece. Sparta to be precise. But why am I seeing this place?

The focus of these images shifts to a lone giant man, working as a blacksmith. Sharpening something, by the look of flying sparks bouncing around. He is happy. Content. A smile, grinning from ear to ear.

I see his work… A sword. Wait, it's 'The' sword. The very

same that almost cut me in half earlier in the night.

It's clear who this individual is now. It's Herakles. But this can't be the cannibalistic monster that attacked me. He seems different. The air is not boiling in his presence. I don't feel any anger or animosity coming from him. Just pure joy and peace with himself.

After his work, Herakles trotted up a stone path to a lone house overlooking Sparta on a hill. It was small but manageable in size. Truth be told, I wondered how a man of his size could fit in there. Suddenly, two small children, a boy and a girl, rushed out of the open entrance in ecstasy and greeted the man. He picked both of them up and embraced them, letting out joyful laughter like Santa Claus.

A woman, who looks about eight months pregnant, stands idly by in the doorway. Herakles puts down his children and kisses the woman in the doorway.

This must be his family.

Another flash. It's raining. Storm clouds have gathered. Thunder and lightning are accompanied by the sounds of war. It is not the peaceful meadows of Sparta I am seeing now. It's the cold and sharp wintery abode of the mountains of Thermopylae. This is where the three hundred Spartans fought back the Persian empire.

Contrasting the Spartans' gold and red attire, the Persians wore brown and grey, making the battle easy to track from my spiritual position as an observer.

Among the ringing sounds of steel and war cries of men, I see Herakles in the fray. His sheer strength and size proving superior to the Persians' war machines and numbers. He is carrying his sword in one hand and a shield in the other. Enemy soldiers are sent flying when struck with the flat of his blade and sawed in half when cut.

At the head of the Spartans, was King Leonidas. It's surreal to watch this living legend. His great spear was alien looking. The metal work more refined and streamlined than anything I've ever seen, even in the modern world. It was also clean and pristine, like it had never been used before. The spear leaves a visible trail as it slices through wind and rain like a trail. I have heard stories of him and his campaign against Persian enslavement. He lives up to his myth and deserves his residing place in history and legends.

But the story of the three hundred can only end as history deems. One by one, red and gold fell into the mud and murky water. And soon, so too, did Leonidas fall. His body stabbed by fifteen blades wielded by fifteen soldiers, all at once into his back. A butterfly of piercing steel.

Seeing his King fall, Herakles charged into the fifteen soldiers and ripped them apart. He held his dying king in his arms. Cradling him like a child. Leonidas whispered into his ear…

"I bequeath you my spear." He held out his arm, still clenching his spear as tightly as he would have at his best.

Herakles took the spear.

"It'll give you great power. Never betray it…" And with those cryptic words. Leonidas passed on.

Flash. I'm back in Sparta. It was night and the moon was full. Herakles watched the horizon with unease from atop a remote cliff, the spear sheathed on his back, alongside his sword.

"Your legend grows, Herakles." A hooded stranger approached from the darkness. Herakles took both weapons hand in hand.

"You know of me, stranger?" he questioned

"Oh yes, we hear tell of the mighty Herakles. The man who cannot be killed, wielding sword and spear. The common folk claim you are the son of Zeus himself."

The stranger paces slowly and wobbly towards a small rock and sits upon it.

"The Persian army grows closer, and soon all of Greece shall be ruled by the mad king Xerxes," he continued.

"Who are you, old man?"

After a brief pause, the stranger replied.

"I am simply the Gravedigger." The old man bows.

Herakles sheathed his weapons. This old man clearly could do no harm to him.

"Be gone, gravedigger, I have battle plans to make," he ordered like a general.

"How to stop the Persians from destroying Sparta?"

"The dead need graves, old man, perhaps you should go back to your profession."

"I can help you."

"I don't need your help."

The old man sighed.

"A shame. I offered my services to Leonidas too, but now he is dead. Died in your arms, correct?"

The air bubbles with heat. A wave of anger befalls the lone warrior. He storms to the gravedigger and wraps his fingers around the old man's thin, bony throat.

"I have told no one that tale. I was the only survivor from that massacre. How could you know this?" Herakles snapped at the man whose life he held betwixt his fingers.

In the blink of an eye, the man disappears from the giant's grasp, leaving nothing but his raggedy old brown cloak in his place. Herakles, stunned, surveys his surroundings with a hint of panic.

"There is more to the world than the arrogant, narrow-minded view of Olympus, my friend."

Herakles looks up, to see the old gravedigger, still cloaked in the same fashion sitting on a perched rock point higher up the mountain. The gravedigger hops off and floats down gracefully to the ground, as if he has wings.

As the man's feet touch the Earth, Herakles draws his weapons once more.

"What are you?"

"I told you. I am the Gravedigger." He bows once more.

"What do you want?"

The old man sighs again. His patience wearing thin.

"Are you listening, boy? I told you I want to help you."

"Why?"

The gravedigger begins to pace towards Herakles.

"I do hate seeing our kind, so troubled, so forgotten, so discarded, and at such a young age as well."

"'Our kind?" Herakles' ears prick up.

The old man, seeing that he has got his attention, waves his finger in the air like he is telling a child off for misbehaving.

"Ah, ah, for context to your question, you must pay."

"Why should I?"

The old man gets to a blade's distance to the disgruntled warrior. The tip resting on his visible ribcage, looking like it is about to puncture him.

"I know who you are. Who you really are. Which Gods are in your favour. Which are not. And I can give you the power to save all of Greece from damnation."

Herakles' face shows he is thinking and contemplating this

ultimatum. He knows this 'gravedigger' has power, he's seen it with his own eyes.

"How many drachma do you want?" He concludes his thinking.

"I have no need for currency, boy. My price is that."

The Gravedigger raises his arm, joints and bones clicking and cracking, and points his skeletal finger at Leonidas' spear.

Herakles looks at the great weapon, the significance of this spear is without question. It belongs to a Spartan. It is a symbol of their power. But to save Greece. His family. Tradition and honour must be cast aside.

He holds out the spear for the man to take. The gravedigger wraps his fingers around the grip like snakes. He takes it and holds it in his hand. Laughing maniacally at great pleasure to his new tool being added to his arsenal.

The sky begins to shake and lightning is being cast and struck in every which way direction, like it's angry and erratic.

The gravedigger looks at Herakles, finished with his victory dance and celebration.

"I am truly sorry for what is to come, my boy."

"What?"

Suddenly, Herakles shrieks in pain and collapses to the floor. Screaming and crying whilst rolling in the mud. The pain shifts to his chest. It begins to turn red, and erupts in flame. The fires wrap around his chest like vines, suffocating him. Like they were drawing something. The fires die. And on his chest, is a branded image of an eagle, still smoking and ash crying off his skin.

More flashes and I hear the repeated dying words of Leonidas…

"Never betray it."

"Never betray it."

"Never betray it."

The words repeat and echo like a broken record, bouncing music and sounds, in a cave. Suddenly, a new voice pierces through the veil. A woman's voice…

"There you are!"

The images I see now are unfocused, erratic, but I spy Herakles clenching his head in pain. Another is the Persian fleet sinking in a hurricane. The waves crashing on the decks and splitting them in two.

It seems the strange old man held up his end of the bargain. But I don't see him in my flashes again. The images stop, showing Herakles knelt down in his house. The entrance door broke. Swinging on its hinges. A trail of blood trickling out. I look closer. There are bodies on the floor. I look closer still. Oh God, his family. His wife and children were like hollowed corpses. Internals scooped out like ice cream.

As if he could sense my presence through time, Herakles slowly turned his head as if he were in a horror movie, facing me. His eyes mad with killer instinct. A lump of human flesh, an organ perhaps, or two, were hanging from his jaws. He was eating his family.

I feel like screaming. A proper scream of sheer fear.

More flashes envelop me again. I feel the ride will soon be over. I see Herakles bowing before a golden statue of King Eurystheus, who when he was still alive, was said to be in commune with the Gods and was frequently invited to dinner parties and banquets in Olympus. He seeks forgiveness for his sins and asylum, now that he has been banished from Sparta. The statue speaks…

"The Sky Father Zeus, your own blood, will cleanse you of

your sin and madness. But to earn his favour, you must complete twelve tasks, each more difficult than the last. Show him your strength and resilience, and he will set you free of your nightmares."

More images flood me, like as if I were watching a montage of events.

Herakles slaying the Nemean Lion. He skins it and adopts the pelts into his armour. He eats the remains and drinks its blood.

The slaying of an enormous Hydra. A serpent like beast with the ability to grow two more heads if one is chopped off.

The capturing of the Golden Hind of Artemis. An animal that looked like an Oryx. And the capture of a giant boar.

Cleaning the Augean stables. He eyed the horses with a deadly thirst.

Slaying the giant Stymphalian Hawks. He ate all but one.

Obtaining a trophy of the Cretan Bull. He ripped off both horns and wore a necklace out of them.

Ending the tyrannical reign of King Diomedes. The king had trained his horses to eat human flesh and ruled his province with an iron fist. Herakles fed the king to the stallions before eating them in turn himself.

Steal the girdle of Hippolyta, the queen of the Amazons.

Steal the cattle of the Monster Geyron, a green skinned giant with three heads and six arms.

Slay the dragon Ladon, who had stolen an apple tree from the Gods.

Finally, he had to steal the giant three headed wolf, Cerberus.

Herakles returned to the statue, with trophies from his quests and presented them to the statue. Only silence is heard back whilst Herakles eagerly awaits judgement.

"The Sky Father, has judged you… guilty!"

Herakles heart sank with sorrow. His eyebrows turned inward and down.

"What?" he shouted. "I completed every task that was given to me!"

"True, but the ulterior motive to these labours was for you to show restraint and control your ravenous hunger. You frequently used violence and brutality to accomplish your goals. The ways of a mortal." The statue spoke with a sombre tone.

Herakles sinks further into the ground, onto his knees. He bows further, placing his forehead on the ground and begs.

"Please. Please. Free me."

"No."

"Then kill me!"

But the statue spoke no more.

Suddenly, I'm taken back to the present, but I see Herakles perspective of the day. After crossing paths with me. He returns to his home. A damp cave off the Jurassic Coast. Hounded by wave after wave, no sane man would dare enter the cave. But Herakles was no sane man. Inside, were paintings, more like scratches, of all the adventures that Herakles had been on. They were rough and primitive like cave paintings of old. A few candles, perched along at select points for optimal light. A fire was simmering in the middle, with a rack of fish cooking above it. A chest filled with currency from across the globe and a pile of clothes in the corner. At the end of his cave was a mural. Dedicated to his deceased family. It was adorned with flowers and some more rough sketches to personify them.

He flings off his civilian clothes, baring himself as nature intended.

He etches a symbol into the ground with his nails. The sound more unbearable than chalk on a whiteboard. The symbol itself was the 'omega' sign. It began to glow.

"I have found the Godslayer," He spoke to the enchanting light.

I open my eyes and I'm back on the train. My mouth agape with drool pouring out like I'm some untrained toddler. To the outside world, I must have looked as if I was sleeping.

"HMM, INTERESTING."

"What? What's interesting?" I wipe my mouth after I speak.

"YOU HAVE BEEN FOUND, DANTE."

"Found? By who?"

"GODS."

The train begins to silently slow to a stop. I look outside and see the tall towers of London and neon lights shining like stars. Waterloo station was where we were stopping at.

"Okay, okay. I've played along enough. Who or what are you really?"

"I AM YOU."

"Funny. Who are you really?"

"ALLOW ME TO CLARIFY, I AM THE COLLECTIVE MEMORIES, WISDOM AND EXPERIENCE OF YOUR PAST LIVES, OR OUR PAST LIVES IF YOU WANT TO LOOK AT IT THAT WAY."

'This must be a joke' I think to myself.

"I ASSURE YOU THIS IS NO JOKE OR JEST."

It can hear my thoughts. It's like a parasite.

"Okay. Why can we communicate now? And not at any point at all in the past? It would have been nice to have some otherworldly wisdom at some points in my life," I hastily say.

"THE MEDICATION, OMNITOXIKE, IT SUPPRESSED OUR CONNECTION. IT WAS ONLY EARLIER TODAY THAT I SYNTHESISED THE CORRECT CHEMICALS TO BALANCE OUT THE TOXIN."

"Chemicals?"

"GAMMA AND VITA RADIATION."

I feel my heart actually stop for a brief moment. These chemicals are radioactive. Dangerous. And they're coursing through my veins and arteries as if they were life preserving blood.

"Are you trying to kill me?" I shout.

I don't look, but I can feel the other passengers gaze in the back of my head. Peeking their heads from behind the seats to take a look at a freak. Burning me with judgement. To be honest, I'd judge me too.

"HOW DARE YOU?" The voice shouts even louder back. Albeit in my head still.

My hand suddenly slaps me across the face. Out of my control. The connection of palm and cheek were loud.

"Did you just slap me?"

"I AM THE ONLY REASON YOU ARE STILL ALIVE."

I feel the sensation of control coming back to my hand.

"THE BIOLOGY OF THE GODSLAYER IS FAR MORE ADVANCED THAN A STANDARD MORTAL, THE RADIATION IS NON-LETHAL TO YOU, I ASSURE. BESIDES IT IS ONLY TEMPORARY."

The control of my hand is suddenly ripped away from me again. My finger extends and points to the nape of my neck.

"THE TOXIN IS MOST POTENT HERE, AT THE NAPE AND EXTENTS DOWN THE SPINE, RENDERING YOUR HEIGHTENED SENSES AND STRENGTH NULLIFIED.

AVOID ANY HARMFUL STIMULI TO THE NECK, OR THE RADIATION WILL BE INTERRUPTED AND OUR CONNECTION WILL BE SEVERED AGAIN. THE TOXIN WILL SPREAD ONCE MORE. AND I CANNOT PROTECT YOU. LIKE I SAID, IT IS ONLY TEMPORARY, AND WHEN ALL OF THE OMNITOXIKE IS OUT OF YOUR SYSTEM, OUR CONNECTION WILL BE PERMANENT AND CANNOT BE BROKEN."

I take a moment to take all of this information in. Godslayers? Past Lives? Toxic medication? It's not every day you get told stuff like this.

"So, someone was trying to stop us with those omnitoxike tablets then?"

"NOW YOU ARE ASKING THE RIGHT QUESTIONS."

"My doctor prescribed them to me, could she have known?"

"WE WILL GET TO THE BOTTOM OF THIS CONSPIRACY AND STOP THE GODS FROM HAUNTING US."

"Thank you, by the way, for everything. I wouldn't be alive if you didn't step in."

"YOU'RE WELCOME."

The train pulls up at Waterloo. The doors open and the passengers begin to disembark.

"What should I call you anyway? It would make things a lot easier."

"CONSIDERING YOUR NAME AND HOW I AM YOUR GUIDE THROUGH THIS NEW WEIRD, WILD AND WICKED WORLD… CALL ME VIRGIL."

Virgil. That was the name of the angel who guided Dante through the nine circles of hell in the poem *Dante's Inferno*. Dante was searching for his wife. Not too dissimilar to what I am doing now. It's not half bad a name, considering his position.

As I disembark the train, heading for the exit doors, I spy a couple watching a video on their phones. Being nosy, I take a cheeky look. The footage horrifies me. The title reads 'Real life superhero fight'. It's a mixture of CCTV footage and captured video on phone cameras of my earlier fight with Herakles. Oh fuck.

Chapter 5

The Bride in Black

Waterloo station was teeming with nightlife and chatter. All manner of people could be seen either eagerly and joyfully venturing out into the big wide city, or returning back wasted, drunk and bad mistakes with spew spread across their shirts like scars.

My destination was Devil's Little Sinners. It was the new nightclub that had just opened in Southwark. It wasn't worth getting an underground ticket. It was only a fifteen-minute walk.

As I walk through the crowds, I notice that more and more people are watching that video, and showing it to others, even random people who cross their paths. It was going viral!

"What do we do Virgil?" I say to myself. A worried tone consistent.

"NOTHING, THIS IS THE WAY OF THE WORLD NOW. THE INTERNET IS A MARVELLOUS INVENTION."

"This isn't going away."

"TAKE SOME ADVICE FROM SOMEONE WHO HAS OVER A MILLION YEARS OF HIVE MIND KNOWLEDGE IN THEIR COLLECTIVE HYPOTHETICAL CRANIUM."

"What?"

"CHILL. OUT. DUDE."

I was now in the city, busy as ever. Loud as ever. An epicentre of chaos. Cars honking. Streets bustling. Neon shining like Christmas on signs and billboards. I saw a pair of individuals whom I assume don't actually know each other (and probably on something) were arguing in the street. About doughnuts.

"This is a shit doughnut," the calmer one said.

I was only a few feet away, a few steps at most, when the more extroverted one shouted.

"It's a good fucking doughnut!"

I think my ears were ringing for a bit.

"So what actually am I? You said something about a Godslayer?" I ask Virgil.

"THE GODSLAYER IS A WARRIOR THAT STANDS AGAINST THE EVIL OF GODS."

"But aren't Gods good?" It's like I'm in school talking to a teacher again.

"NO, FAR FROM IT. THROUGHOUT HISTORY, GODS DEMAND SACRIFICE, LIKE DEATH, BLOOD, VIRGINS, TO APPEASE THEIR SEXUAL FETISHES. ETERNAL DEVOTION OTHERWISE YOU'LL BE DAMNED TO WHATEVER VERSION OF HELL YOU BELIEVE IN, NOT TAKING INTO CONSIDERATION IF YOU ARE GOOD OR NOT. THEY SCHEME TO TAKE OVER THE WORLD AND COSMOS, USING DARK SORCERY, BLACK MAGIC OR CURSED POWERS, BELIEVING THEMSELVES TO BE THE ONE TRUE RULER AMONGST OTHERS. THAT'S WHERE YOU COME IN. TO STOP THEM FROM RUINING SPACE AND TIME," Virgil passionately speaks.

"Any examples of these dastardly plans?" I casuistically question.

"1656 YEARS AFTER THEIR EMERGENCE, THE WORLD IS FLOODED BY THE CHRISTIAN GOD.

“250 BC, THE GODS HORUS, SOBEK AND ANUBIS SEEK TO HARNESS AND ENSLAVE THE POWER OF THE SUN, AFTER MURDERING THEIR FATHER RA, THE GOD OF THE SUN, IN HIS SLEEP.

“NINTH CENTURY, THE NORSE GODS SEEK TOTAL WORLD DOMINATION AND SERVITUDE, BY INFLUENCING THEIR SUBJECTS, THE VIKINGS, TO SAIL WEST TO NEW LANDS.”

“Okay. I get it.”

The nightclub was vibrant and exotic compared to the rest of London’s nightly establishments. Red headlights were beaming, celebrating its extravagance. The logo featured a sexy woman, dressed in 1950s clothes, and a little demon, looking like a Gremlin, with a cheeky grin, was lifting her skirt, trying to expose her butt. The woman’s face was a mixture of shock and pleasure. How tacky.

“THIS PLACE LOOKS LIKE A SHITHOLE,” Virgil’s deep monstrous voice comments. I couldn’t help but agree.

Strobe beams and dimly lit red lights made it difficult to navigate the floor. The staff were dressed in tuxedos for men and red scaly dresses for women, all whilst wearing devil horns on their heads. The guests were all very attractive. Models, supermodels, Hollywood actors, they were all here and in plentiful quantity. Some even dressed to the theme.

“LOOK AT ALL THESE WEIRDOS.”

The music stalled for a moment, everyone was displeased, but then the all too familiar opening chime of ‘Never Gonna Give You Up’ by Rick Astley, began to beat and the crowd laughed and danced it off like it was all part of the plan. We just got Rick Rolled.

I frantically searched for Mia. She wasn't on the dance floor. Nor were Clyde or Regina. I wasn't much of a dancer to begin with, so navigating through the jumping and erratically dancing adults was most annoying.

"DANTE, OVER YONDER." I could still hear Virgil, even over the loud speaker amplified music.

He was directing me to the VIP booths. There she was, as well as Clyde and Regina. And Bob Chase. A small and tubby man, who would use money to solve all of his problems. He was getting way too friendly with Mia for my comfort. His arms were wrapped around her and he was speaking directly into her ear. Her giggling to his comments. I'm not the jealous type, but I really don't have time for this.

"Mate, you made it!" Clyde jumps out of his seat and hugs me. Still holding a glass of wine in one hand.

"There you are!" Mia follows suit and kisses me, I can smell the alcohol on her breath. She is drunk.

"Dante!" Regina shouts my name joyfully, like welcoming someone who has been gone for a very long time.

Bob stands up and rebuttons his jacket, then extends his hand courteously.

"You must be Dante Adler, Mia's other half." I shake his hand, but I don't think I like this guy.

"FUCK THIS GUY. It seems neither does Virgil.

"Your wife has kept us company with wonderful stories, Dante, like the girl who stuck a cucumber up herself. The dopy tart." The gang laughs to his comment. Even Mia, whose friend he is besmirching.

"I'm sure they're all fun, fun, fun, but I need to talk—"

Whoa, my dude. What has happened to your clothes?" Bob cuts me off.

It was inevitable that my appearance would be brought up. The cut threads could be seen even in this poor light.

"I fell." I lie and brush it off like an annoying fly.

"PISS POOR EXCUSE. NO ONE WILL BUY THAT."

"Oh God, I'm so sorry," Regina sympathetically says.

"WHAT?"

"Anyway as I was saying Mia and I really should go." I try to signal to Mia, but she is too busy laughing and chugging down champagne. Suddenly Virgil chips in like an alarm clock…

"OH SHIT, DANTE!"

"Not now."

"Who are you talking to, mate?" Clyde states. Confused by my newfound habit of talking to myself.

"TWELVE O'CLOCK, TWELVE O'CLOCK!" Virgil sounds agitated and worried. He wasn't like this when we were up against Herakles. Much more confident and filled with bravado. Now he is like a scared cat.

"I don't care about what time it is."

"Are you okay? Hit your head too hard perhaps?" Bob butts in, clearly not caring about the sarcastic tone in his dreary voice.

"Shut up, Bob!" I shout back. Losing my cool suave.

"Whoa, whoa." Mia finally comes back to reality.

"DANTE!"

"Everybody shut up!" I shout at the top of my lungs like a screeching hawk. I didn't even realise that the music had stopped whilst in the heat of the moment. Everyone was looking at one person. Me. But then I spot what Virgil was warning me about. He meant twelve o'clock as in 'behind me'.

A woman. No. A corpse. Dressed in a black wedding dress. Holding a bouquet of dead and withered flowers in her hands. A strange oil or tar-like substance enveloped her body and was leaking off her like water to the ground. Her face shrouded by a veil.

Not long after, everybody else noticed her. Dropping their glasses of alcoholic beverages in stun and gasping in fear and bewilderment. Bob Chase steps forward…

"Who the bloody hell are you?"

The bride says nothing. We could only hear her breathing, like a cold and callous intake and exasperated and fragile outtake.

"Right, enough of this shit." He signals to his security. "Remove this skank from my club."

Two big and burly brutes in security black shirts waddle over to the intruder.

The bride sucks in a deep intake of air, like a vacuum… And screeches it out like a banshee. The pitch was deafening and explosive. Every glass and window shattered into a million tiny pieces. The guests fell to the floor, clutching their ears with fountains of blood squirting out of their ear canals. No scream could be heard over the banshee cry.

I fall to the floor, but my ears are not hurting as much by the looks of the others. No blood was pouring nor even dripping out. But I did get cut by a loose shard of glass across my arm. I pulled up what remained of my jacket to look at the gaping wound.

My skin around the cut was grey and pale, like a vampire. The wound quickly stitched itself back together and my normal complexion returned.

The banshee ceased her cry. I looked around, everyone was on the floor, bleeding out. Painting the wooden boards of the dance floor red like art on a canvas.

Mia was passed out, her ears still bleeding, but not as frequently or dramatically as the others. I pick her up like a damsel in distress and make way for the fire exit. My balance was off kilter and it was hard trying to walk normally and straight.

Just as I open the exit doors, leading into an alley with garbage and wasted confection wrapper and rats, I feel a sharp sting in my nape and stumble to the ground, defenceless. This is exactly what Virgil warned me about. Now that I've been struck there, I'm temporarily mortal once more until Virgil can synthesise the radiation and reconnect us. My healed injuries begin to reappear too. Cuts and bruises scarred me like shame. I tumble into the big blue garbage bin and drop Mia. I drop to the floor and rest against the bin. Taking Mia and holding her close to me. I pull the stinger out from my neck. It was one of the dead flowers. A rose. It had been thrown like an acupuncture needle straight into the nerve in my neck.

The bride stood before us with murderous intent. Her heels clicking against the stone as she slowly paced toward us like a predator that had caught her prey.

She knelt down before us. I held Mia as tightly as I could. I knew this was the end, and accepted this fact.

The bride raised her sharp talons for fingers. She slings them towards me like a cat catching a small bird. I close my eyes, awaiting release. But nothing happens. I begin to open them. Her claws are mere millimetres from my face. Her face showing an actual emotion. Fear. Her body was wrapped around in blue chains like tendrils, that seem to be hanging from the sky with no anchoring point. Keeping her in place and paralysed like a statue in a Church graveyard. The chains yank her upward and she goes flying towards the sky. Her body disintegrates into smoke and the lifesaving chains disappear too. I sigh in relief and soon begin to drift off to dreamland. Falling fast asleep.

What a day. I am so tired.

Chapter 6

Clover

"Sir? Are you okay?" A policewoman was standing over me like a guardian angel and gently shrugging me awake. Or to see if I was still breathing. One or the other.

The sounds of sirens were ringing like familiar church bells in the dark. It was still night. So I assume I must have been out for not even an hour if the police have shown up.

My bloodshot eyes observe the area. I don't see Mia.

"Where… Where is she?" I struggle to force the words out and struggle to stand on my own two feet. The officer catches me and hoists me up.

"The woman you were with is fine. She's been taken to St Esta's Hospital, for a doctor to look over her for any more injuries."

It was only now that I realised that I couldn't hear the 'other' voice in my head. Virgil must still be working to fix our severed connection after the Bride hit me.

The officer helped me to the front of the club where the paramedics and boys in blue were waiting. Yellow police tape encompassed the whole area like a quarantine zone. It was just like one of those police shows on the TV. A crowd of pedestrians were eagerly trying to get a peek and snapshot at what was going on.

There were rows upon rows of body bags placed on the floor

in a neat orderly line.

"Did anyone else make it?"

"No, you and the other woman are the only survivors."

I can't believe that. My friends were dead. Killed by that creature in black. If only I wasn't there. Perhaps everyone would still be alive. At least Mia is alive and being looked after. I should visit as soon as I can.

Not long after, a paramedic tends to my wounds, stitching the cuts on my forehead and arm. Two men in dark blue suits, one with a thick brown moustache, walk up to me.

"Dante Adler, my name is Agent Tom Grayson, this is my colleague Agent Harry Lyle. We'd like to ask a few questions about what transpired here tonight." He speaks in a thick American accent, like he is from Texas.

I don't meet his eye line or even acknowledge his comment, but am still listening. Harry takes out a cigarette and lighter from his jacket pocket and lights it and begins to huff and puff like the big bad wolf. These guys are standard stereotypes for cops. I'm half expecting the other one to pull out a doughnut and begin to chow down.

Tom tries to reach me again. "If you would come with us please, sir."

I look up, finally meeting his gaze, but look down again. I nod in agreement to his request.

They drove me to Scotland Yard. I didn't speak to them, but during the trip I overheard a crucial conversation between the agents.

"Country's going to shit, Tom. We got the Hulk tearing up part of Guildford and now a sonic attack with no evidence. We are living the movies now," Harry spoke in a Northern accent.

I sat in the back seat and those key words 'Hulk' and 'Guildford' pricked my ears up. I look forward. I see through the protective plastic shielding of the front and back seat, as this was a police car, that they both have black four leafed clovers tattooed on one side of their necks. Curious.

"Take a seat." Tom points me to a steel chair tucked under a metal table. This was an interrogation room. It had the one-way glass panel as well. A lone security camera was tucked high in the corner, blinking a small red light every five seconds to show it was recording. The whole room was a tapestry of grey. My hair was the only exotic colour that brightened this dull, dreary and depressing room.

We both sit at opposite ends of the cold table. The agent pulls out a pen and notebook.

"What do you remember in the nightclub?"

I was about to answer until…

"DON'T SPEAK." Virgil was once again prowling and poking around inside my head like an old friend. Or a brain surgeon.

"IF YOU SPEAK, MY PROGRESS WILL BE UNDONE. I'M NEARLY FINISHED. GIVE ME A FEW MORE MINUTES."

I sit still in silence. Tom writes a note and looks to the security camera briefly. It blinks. He turns back to me.

"Anyone of interest?"

I say nothing.

Tom turns to the camera again as if it were an OCD habit. The red light does not blink again. Tom turns to me.

"Godslayer."

My heart can't take many more of these plot twists as it briefly pauses with shock. How does he know about the Godslayer? Does he know everything? Still I say nothing. I may need Virgil's help in a bit.

"Allow me to clarify. I imagine your 'inner voice' is asking you to remain silent?"

I nod in response to his question.

"DON'T!" Virgil snaps back like an angry dog on a leash.

"Okay." Tom writes a note. "Dante, my associate Agent Lyle has disabled all CCTV footage here allowing us to speak freely about these supernatural topics. I'm part of an organisation that wants the same things that you do. We are Clover. Protecting the world against supernatural and Godly threats. We believe they have found you. You're marked."

I want to ask so many questions, but I doubt Virgil will want to cooperate with whoever these guys are.

"We have also deduced that you are the individual that was fighting Herakles in Guildford earlier this evening. That can remain a secret, or be in the public domain. The choice is up to you. We have the power to hush this story."

I don't like the sound of this. Are they blackmailing me?

"My organisation would like to propose a truce. An alliance to stop these current threats. Help us, slayer. We can protect you and your family."

"ASK HIM WHAT HE MEANS BY 'TRUCE'." Virgil has given me the go to speak. Our connection must be secure.

"Truce?" I snarl back.

Tom seems to be taken aback by my statement.

"I guess there are no secrets between you and your past lives is there? I'll be honest me and my organisation were hoping the connection wasn't strong enough for this level of psychic symbiosis. We have occasionally been on opposite sides of the war. You are a third party. A thorn in our side, that must be removed from time to time." Tom says this whilst gritting his teeth together, like he's holding back anger.

"THEY WILL LOCK YOU UP, AND USE YOU AS BAIT. THEY HAVE BEFORE."

After much thought. Contemplating pros and cons. I think…

"This isn't for me. I got no beef with your organisation, so just let me go," I ask.

Tom is visibly angry. He slams his fist on the table in a fit of unbridled rage. He laughs like a man who has lost all his bargaining chips in a gamble. Maniacal, and yet still methodical. Still thinking of his next move. All in? Cash out? Or bring out the big guns?

"Perhaps Omnitoxike is not such a fruitful labour after all. You're still as stubborn as ever."

My arm and hand reaches out and slaps the agent across his cheek. Making a large slapping sound. Tom goes flying into the direction of the forceful hit into the wall. His limp body slides down like a slab of butter against the wall and finally reaches the grey floor tiles. A large red handprint was stained across his face.

My own hand feels like it's on fire or an extreme version of rope burn. I shake it as if I'm fanning out a fire.

"What is it with you and slapping?" I talk to Virgil. He doesn't reply to this remark and instead begins his drill Sergeant role once again…

"PICK UP HIS PHONE."

I rummage through his pockets and eventually, I got it! A grey iPhone 12. Someone doesn't want to upgrade it seems.

"CRUSH IT."

I squeeze the device between my fingers. It splinters and

breaks into chunks of circuitry and glass. It doesn't hurt. It feels like knowledge. Like a key to a vault. Looking at my palm, I see what remains of the phone be absorbed into my skin like melting chocolate. My whole arm feels like it's tingling and a similar sensation to pins and needles. It spreads up my arm and all the way to my brain. I hear codes. Numbers. I don't understand.

"What was that?"

"NOW WE HAVE ACCESS TO SECURE RADIO FREQUENCIES USED BY CLOVER. YOU ABSORBED THE INFORMATION. THAT'S WHAT WE CAN DO. PSYCHOMETRY. WITNESSING AN OBJECT'S HISTORY AND INFO. CONGRATULATIONS, DANTE, YOU ARE THE FIRST HUMAN RADIO TOWER."

"We can use this to overhear police scanners and anything that would be of interest to Clover and therefore us."

"NOW YOU'RE CATCHING ON."

I can now feel the connection between us growing. All this locked and broken wisdom is starting to piece itself together again. Like a jigsaw that was missing a piece, only to find that you were holding it all along.

I crack my knuckles and shake my hands. I bet I look like an action star.

"He mentioned my medication. It seems the plot thickens."

"WORRY ABOUT HOW WE'RE GONNA GET OUT OF HERE."

I can't help but pull a smug face. As if anyone will actually see it.

"Watch this."

Not five minutes later, I walk out the front door. No questions asked. No bloody battle or daring escape covered by gunfire and smoke. Just casual strides and good times.

"I THOUGHT THERE WOULD BE SOME SORT OF BATTLE OR SOMETHING. I MEAN, WE DID KNOCK SOMEONE OUT."

"You knocked someone out. The CCTV was cut off. No one knows what happened. You've watched too many movies."

"I'VE SEEN THE SAME NUMBER OF MOVIES AS YOU HAVE! IT'S NOT LIKE I CAN GO ANYWHERE."

There was a chill in the air. The breeze was cold and uninviting. Even the city was not as lively as it was earlier. It must be midnight by now.

"So then. What now?" I sternly speak with confidence.

"NOW, WE CAN DO WHATEVER WE WANT."

Chapter 7

The Blood Whips

Let's recap shall we?

I'm the latest in a long line of reincarnations known as The Godslayer. A super powered warrior that stands against evil and saves the world like some B movie action man from supernatural monsters and threats. Particularly Gods.

It also comes with Virgil. The collective experience and knowledge of my past lives. Here to train me, acting like the Master Yoda to my Luke Skywalker. He also never shuts up and constantly shouts at me. And occasionally rips the controls of my body.

I've only learnt this recently because it turns out the medication Omnitoxike, which I used to supress my migraines, was actually poisoning me and repressing my powers.

So far the only lead as to the why or whom of poisoning me is a shadowy organisation called Clover. They also don't seem to like me.

You know who else doesn't like me? Herakles. The bastard son of Zeus. Turns out the Disney movie of Hercules is a bunch of bullshit, because in reality, he is a raging, hulking and cannibalistic monster who looks like He-Man.

There is also my ability to extract information from objects. Oh, and there's another monster that's pursuing me that I've dubbed The Bride in Black, that attacked the club I was at and has currently put my wife in the hospital.

That sums it up. Or do I need to go further than the past few hours? No. Why, you might ask? Because now, I can do whatever I want. And I want some god damn food.

I find a twenty-four-seven McDonalds by London bridge, next to the towering Shard. I actually usually hate the McDonalds breakfast. The McMuffin for example tastes like wet blankets and crusty toenails in my personal opinion. But now, as I shove the breakfast burger down my gullet, it tastes like pulled pork, slow roasted on a spit. Seasoned with spices perfectly like it was cooked in a five-star restaurant and personally overseen by Gordon Ramsey.

The time was 1.23 a.m. October 30th. One day to Halloween. But you could've fooled me. My life lately has been nothing but horrors and jump scares.

I take a swig of the bottle of milk I purchased with the meal. It tastes like a fine aged wine from 1957. Screw the Savoy grill. Perhaps I should just eat here for the best meals in the city.

Just as I enjoy my moment of peace and quiet, a word all in capitals lights up in bulging capital letters. Not like when Virgil speaks in all caps, no this was different, like this is my idea.

"Weapon?"

That's it! That's what I need to even out the playing field. A weapon. Herakles has a sword. The bride has her weird flower knives. I need one of my own.

"Hey V, do you—"

"DID YOU JUST CALL ME V?" He cuts me off midsentence like scissors through paper, or a knife through butter.

"Can I not call you that?"

"NO."

"It would make things quicker. It's like a nickname. Or a codename."

"NO."

"If I can call you V, you can call me Dan."

"HOW ABOUT I CALL YOU ASSHOLE AND MAKE IT SQUAT!"

Okay, I can see this is going nowhere. Codenames can be scratched off of the many imaginary queries I have in my imaginary notebook.

"Anyway…" I begin awkwardly "Is there a weapon or something that you might know about that we can get quick access to in the city?"

"WHAT? LIKE SOME SORT OF SWORD?"

"Well, yeah."

Virgil laughs. It sounds sort of what I'd imagine an ox would sound like if they had the vocal cords and muscles in their face to do this. Kind of like a supervillain's laugh as well. Like Willem Dafoe's Green Goblin from the *Spider-Man* movies. A weird combo I know.

"DON'T SOUND SO NAÏVE. YOU THINK YOU'LL LOOK LIKE A JEDI CLINT EASTWOOD IF YOU GRAB A SWORD? SWING IT AROUND WITH NO PRECISION OR ACCURACY YET STILL HIT EVERY MARK? NO! A SWORD IS SO LIMITING. THINK BIGGER. MORE VERSATILE. MORE VERTICALITY. MORE SPUNK!"

I don't think I've ever heard the word 'spunk' sound so beaten and tacked on before in my life.

"You sound like a disembodied hive mind voice with a plan, Virgil."

"I MAY KNOW OF A TRINKET NEARBY."

I raise my half empty milk bottle like a glass of wine and am about to conduct a toast and cheers with a group of people.

"To tearing shit up?" I remark.

"TO TEARING SHIT UP!"

I imagine a chink of glasses. Despite the fact I'm holding cheap plastic.

Virgil tells me of an old weapon. Forged in the fires of Mount Vesuvius in Pompeii. The tale begins with an old blacksmith named Tarful, who comes from a land so old it is forgotten by history and discarded by time. He tells that Tarful was tasked by the sea god Poseidon, to create a weapon capable of slaying a titan or giant. Tarful was gleeful that the gods chose him to help in their strife against the enemies of foreign realms. He took up shop inside the mountain, as the volcano within was in fact the gravestone of the titan of fire, Perses. In his life, Perses was made of molten rock and lava with stalactites for claws and boulders for muscles, he was capable of blowing hurricanes made of fire with acid hot rain with his breath. He was almost as massive as Atlas himself. Perses met his end from the Norse God of Thunder, Thor. This made the soil of the mountain rich with opportunity for farming, allowing him to build himself a home. The rocks as tough as Mjolnir. And steel as strong as Excalibur.

Tarful used these facets to live a quaint and content life in Pompeii. Making a living selling the strongest weapons whilst forging Poseidon's weapon as well.

And lo and behold, the image of this weapon came to him. Inspiration and passion drenched Tarful like a waterfall in a green lush jungle.

He used the steel from the mountain and forged it in fire. Using anvil and hammer, the clang of metal clashing could ring throughout all of Pompeii.

The final product resembled a pair of centipedes that would wrap around like bracelets. Each was to go on one arm and could grow or shrink to fit the user's size.

Once equipped, the user could summon the blood whips. They were made of the user's blood and bound together with the electricity within the body to keep the shape. Giving the whips some slight electrical characteristics as well, like sparks and red streams crackling off the whips and a chainsaw-like humming.

Unfortunately for Tarful, the lingering spirit of Perses' erupting power, tried to latch onto the weapons as it was forged, to escape his confining grave. The act of this attempt caused the volcano to erupt, leading to the sad truth of Pompeii's fate.

Perses attempt failed, leading to his spirit being exorcised in the process. The fire titan could no longer plot a potential return. The last light of him was snuffed out, like so many candles.

Pompeii was a ghost. A monument of death. With only the petrified statues of the populace left to mark its place.

Tarful perished as well. His work, ashes. Only the centipedes remain. Hidden until they were uncovered by a team of British explorers in the 1950s.

Over time, the centipedes had eroded and preserved themselves into a greying fossilised substance. Leading the explorers into believing them to be a primeval subspecies of the insect that lived millions of years before. And therefore to take them to…

"The Natural History Museum," I comment, as I look at the majesty of the famous building. Founded by a renowned scientist named Richard Owen and dedicated to a man who questioned God, Charles Darwin, the father of evolution. Its red brick is enhanced by the angelic lights that brighten it up in the dark like a shining lighthouse in a sea of black.

I used to love coming here as a kid. Specially to see the dinosaurs. Who didn't love dinosaurs growing up? Giants of the past, basically real-life monsters, from storybooks and fairy tales. Well, that's what I thought the limit of what a monster could be back then.

Now I have to find a way to break in and steal an exhibit.

If I remember correctly, there is a glass skyline that lies above one of the halls. That would be the stealthiest approach. I don't fancy busting down a wall of one of my favourite places as a child. The only issue is, how do I scale up a wall?

I try (pathetically I might add) to try a run up and see where that gets me. Turns out the parkour system of *Assassin's Creed* is not based on real life physics. I land back on the grass with a thud. I can hear the snickering laughter of my 'other'.

"Okay, you got any bright ideas on how to get to the roof?"

"TRY LOOKING AROUND THE CORNER."

And lo and behold. What do I find? Some scaffolding and construction that leads directly to the roof.

"How did you—?"

"LISTEN, DANTE. YOU MUST LISTEN. USE ALL YOUR SENSES. DO NOT ONLY RELY ONLY ON SIGHT. I COULD HEAR THE WIND AND AIR FLOWING THROUGH AND AROUND THE METAL BARS, LIKE A STRANGER CALLING US. I SENSED THE SHAPES. IT WAS NOT DIFFICULT TO DEDUCE WHAT WAS THERE. REMEMBER, YOU ARE NO MERE MORTAL. YOU ARE BETTER. BE BETTER."

The words made me feel great. Like having butterflies and my favourite food whirling around me inside. I should listen to

Virgil more accurately. He is very wise. He is me after all.

There was a lone security guard prowling around the scaffolding. It looked like the builders were working on some of the roof work above. Nothing major, but still they don't want kids to go around leaping from rooftop to rooftop, hence the security.

He was easy to avoid, like a ninja, I snuck past him using my heightened reflexes to dodge out of his eye line when he turned towards me. Hiding behind equipment or boxes. One with the shadows I tried to use the ability to listen to how the wind was turning and bouncing off of objects to pinpoint his location, but I still needed practise. I kept hearing just the regular whistling breeze.

I climbed up the outside of the metal bars like a spider monkey. I didn't use the conventional method of using the ladders as the guard would see me if his patrol pattern and path was anything to go on. At least there were some wooden boards held up to strengthen the construction poles and keep out the wind. They would give me cover as I climbed the outside.

The trips to Go Ape proved fruitful with these hopping and scurrying escapades.

The roof was wet and slippery. Cold and discouraging. The damn snow and rain had made it almost impossible to keep upright and steady. Still I got a semi-decent view from up here.

I found the glass skyline. I looked down. It was only about a ten-metre drop to a hallway below. Hardly a stumble in my experience now.

Of course there was an elephant in the room now, and no I don't mean that there was a model elephant in the room below me. I mean that now I'd have to shatter the glass to slip in. Someone will hear that. I could try to pry it open with my strength, but it still wouldn't be subtle enough. Besides I don't know construction or architecture. Who knows if ripping off a slab of the roof will cause a chain reaction of cracks and damage. Anyone and their deaf grandma would hear that.

"STRUGGLING? IT'S NOT UNCOMMON FOR PERFORMANCE ISSUES TO OCCUR UNDER HIGH LEVELS OF STRESS."

"Shut up! I just don't want to break anything."

"LET ME UNBURDEN YOU."

My fist clenches, rises and thrusts itself into a window panel. Breaking it into I don't even know how many pieces. My body, as if pushed by a ghost, does a forward roll into the newfound entrance. The momentum causes me to do a front flip before I land on my feet on the floor like a gymnast. The creaking and cracking of wood and glass was indeed not very stealthy. Virgil clearly has very little patience.

"What the hell was that?" I shout, but through a whispered and softer filter.

"A DAMM IMPRESSIVE FRONT FLIP IF YOU ASK ME."

"We're supposed to be doing this quietly."

"STEALTH SUCKS. WHAT HAPPENED TO TEARING SHIT UP?"

"I know but—" I catch my breath "You have to show restraint. Be smart. We have been the cause of enough explosions and grief for a while."

"YOU LECTURE ME ABOUT GRIEF AND RESTRAINT?"

"Yes."

"YOU. HAVE NOT GIVEN YOUR FRIENDS' DEATH A SECOND THOUGHT. YOU. ARE THE ONE WHO BLEW UP HERAKLES AND THAT OIL TRUCK. I HAVE BEEN ONLY

DEFENDING YOU!"

The words hit me like a jackhammer. It's true. I forgot all about my friends Clyde and Regina. I was the one who blew up Herakles. I didn't even think if the driver was still inside the truck when I ignited the oil trail. I'll probably never know.

The media call me superhero. But I'm just as cold and callous as these monsters that haunt me.

Suddenly, as I'm deep in thought. I catch a light in my peripheral vision.

"Hands up!" The voice was high pitched. It was a man, but a young man. Probably museum security.

"Turn around. Slowly now."

It seems to me that my life is now taking orders from just about anyone. I do as he asks.

The guard was young. He wore a blue shirt uniform with a navy tie and cap. He was holding a flashlight with the beam directly in my face, and a Taser gun in the other. Ready to fire.

"No way." His tone sounded less formal and more like a fan seeing his favourite celebrity. "You're him. You're the guy. The man in black fighting that giant." The guard put away his flashlight and gun, and was struggling to contain his excitement. He wadded over and shook my hand.

"Barry. Barry Busfak. I'm a huge fan by the way. Your video is just the best." He continued to shake my hand. "I'm shaking your hand too long aren't I?"

I nodded. He let go swiftly and hastily.

"Sorry. It's just not every day you meet a real-life superhero."

"Thanks, but I'm no hero."

"Sure you are. Look." He hastily grabbed his phone out of his trouser pocket and logged onto YouTube. He pulled up my video. It had ninety million views. The comments were definitely 'something'.

Most praised me. They were probably just excited. Some thought the whole thing was Photoshop and edited together in a movie studio. A promotion for a new film maybe. Some even said I was no better than the giant monster I was fighting. Stating, and I quote, 'He clearly has no self-control with his punches or care for the safety of the populace. To him this is just a playground to throw his toys about in'.

Barry closes his phone.

"See man, you're a hero."

"Well, some seem to share your opinion."

I couldn't think what else to say. There was an awkward silence. Barry was still smiling, beaming with joy. I think it was more awkward for me than him.

"Anyway…" I begin. "I gotta go. Superhero stuff, ya know?" I turn my back to him.

"Let me help."

This guy is full of surprises. I turn back to face him. "What?"

"Well, it's just… I always wanted to be a superhero and go on adventures and such." Barry speaks like a proud political speaker. I can hear the motivation in his tone.

After a moment's reprieve. I make up my mind.

"Do you know where a pair of centipedes that were found in Pompeii are being kept?"

Barry's smile stretches even further than should be physically possible. A smile like a Cheshire cat, grinning from ear to ear.

"It would be my genuine pleasure, sir."

Barry escorts me down hallway after hallway. Sometimes it felt like I was trapped in a labyrinth of endlessly rerendered halls and passages. This was all whilst he was telling me about pretty much his whole life story and hopes and dreams. Fears and nightmares. Favourite candy and sports teams. I owed it to him to listen to it all as he was making my life so much easier. Trying to find an animal in this museum is like a miniscule needle in a giant monopoly haystack.

Eventually, Barry stops his momentous stride. We were right outside the insect exhibits.

"They should be in here."

Inside were giant plastic models of bees, wasps, arachnids, millipedes and more. Information boards were scattered about everywhere like dropped chocolate squares. There were rows of menageries showing all the different families of each type of creepy crawly and fluttering flyer. I looked around. Inspecting every damp place and dark corner as well. Eventually, I found the metaphorical golden goose!

Two grey and eroded looking centipedes were shrivelled and curved in a glass display box. They were labelled as 'Voxapedes'.

"Barry! It's here!" I shouted in excitement.

I could hear the rattling and jingling of his equipment as he hopped over in a haste.

"Holy moly!" he said. Each second he seems to be acting more like the Robin to my Batman. Like a sidekick. "How are you going to get them?"

Instantly I smash the glass, reducing the display box to little chips and pebbles.

As I reach out to grasp the centipedes, I can feel electricity spiking off of them. Like a magnetic attraction. The grey corrosive layer begins to flake off like snow, revealing their true golden bronze cast colour. The two metallic objects lunge forward, each wrapping themselves around one of my wrists each like they were watches. The mandibles biting the ends of their bodies and welding shut. Their small legs burrowing into my skin and flesh. They would not be easy to take off.

"What are they?" Barry asks.

"Things that don't belong here," I reply with a cool overtone.

As we walk back to the entrance, another guard watches with a cartoon-like shocked expression dabbed across his swollen face.

"What the fuck, Busfak?" he shouts. This guard was a lot older and bigger around the waist than Barry was.

"Sorry, I should have told you about Jackson," Barry whispers to me.

Jackson rushes over as fast as his fat tubby legs can take him. When he catches up to us, I swear I can see sweat beginning to drip across his brow.

"You can kiss your job goodbye, Busfak!" he berates him. "And as for you, who the fuck are you?"

Before I could answer, Barry had unholstered his Taser gun like a cowboy in a spaghetti western and had shot Jackson point blank in the face. Jackson twitches and falls face first on the cold marble floor.

"I got your back, Man in Black," Barry says whilst holstering his gun with a little trick. This guy was all right in my book.

Barry escorted me to the entrance lobby, also known as Hintze Hall. He had offered to unlock the doors for me, instead of breaking a wall to make a fashionable exit. The lobby's massive halls and giant space echoed our footsteps as we descended down the wide castle-like stairs. Towards the ceiling, hung a massive

Blue Whale skeleton, hovering over us like a bird of prey.

Rows of prehistoric animal skeletons, like mammoths and sabre-toothed tigers were placed on the home stretch towards the locked main entrance gates.

Barry takes out his key chain and after a slight delay in finding the right one, he slides his key into the lock and…

Ching!

The doors were unlocked and open.

"Thank you Barry, you're a kind soul." Barry blushed. "I'm sorry about your job."

"Don't worry about it. Jackson is out cold and I'll just say, if he remembers anyway, who you were and it was a matter of saving someone's life."

I shake Barry's hand with a firm grasp.

"This is the greatest day of my life, sir," Barry cheerfully says.

Slash!

Slash? I look at Barry. His wide eyed jolly happy go lucky smile shrunk. His eyes began to twitch. He coughed a small supplement of blood. I cast my gaze down to his chest. A massive glistening metal blade was stabbed right through Barry's ribcage.

Barry was raised into the air towards the ceiling. I started to see a shape up in the rafters. But as I looked skyward, a small black oily liquid landed on my face. I rub it off and recognise it as the same as the Bride's from earlier.

But the attacker's shape was clear now as it revealed itself from the shadows.

It had the upper body of a man. A giant man. His arms and hands were not there. Instead only connected metal and long sharp swords replaced them. Its waist down, resembled a snake. His whole body was covered in blades and knives, like armour.

Where the armour meets, was where the black liquid was leaking through.

"Was this man bothering you, slayer?" It spoke like a serpent. Putting a harsh emphasis on the 'S' in its speech.

It was then I could see the head. A rotting and decaying skull, still covered in sharp metal pieces, albeit smaller.

"What are you?" I shouted back, trying to hold off a flood of tears.

"Sorry, I shouldn't have just 'cut' in like that." The monster stabbed Barry with its other sword arm and did a pincer movement, slicing Barry in half. Sending his parts flying in opposite directions. A rain of blood stained the room.

The monster slithered down along the walls and pillars towards me, its metallic body clinging and clanging as it moved.

I try to back away, edging slowly to any point of egress I can find, but I bump into something wooden and slimy. Turning around showed me a new horror to face.

A poorly crafted wooden man, who looked like the only thing keeping him upright were loose strings. The puppet wore torn clothes like they were ripped off a homeless person. Its exposed wooden body showed scarring and splinters. The slime was the same black liquid. A pattern was beginning to emerge.

I was trapped, surrounded by the wolves. They circled around me. Hungry for my blood.

"I see you've met Eris, slayer," the blades spoke.

I could feel Virgil twisting the gears in his hive mind trying to deduce who or what these things are. "He's not much of a talker."

So, the wooden one is called Eris. I don't recognise the name from any kind of mythology.

"Allow me to introduce myself…" The blade covered snake

stopped and bowed before me. "I am Apate," it speaks and raises its head.

"Come on, Virgil. Talk to me," I whisper to myself.

Eris hits me with his long arm as if to remind me he's still here and getting impatient. Apate leaps over me and hits Eris with the flat of his sword arm. The blow adds another scar to Eris and chips a splinter off.

"Patience, Brother. He will die soon enough."

My fear was drowning me in a sea of uneasiness. I needed Virgil to save me.

"ACOLYTES," Virgil finally spoke, but he was just as cryptic as ever with his way with words. "THEY ARE THE ACOLYTES OF DEATH. SO TOO WAS THE BRIDE."

Whatever that means.

"How do I use these whips?" I whisper quickly whilst these Acolytes are distracted.

"I DON'T KNOW."

"What do you mean you don't know? You're supposed to know everything!"

"THE WHIPS HAVE NEVER BEEN USED. THEY WERE BURIED REMEMBER."

He was right. In the story, as soon as they were forged by Tarful, Vesuvius erupted and they were buried under mountains of ash. I had to improvise. Quick.

The beings of black turned to me and edged ever closer and closer, foam starting to form in their mouths like hungry rabid dogs.

I tried to do the rock star hand sign. Nothing.

Thumbs up? Nothing.

Middle finger? Nothing.

Peace sign? Nothing.

Finally, I tried to clench my fist and simulate a punching momentum. Nothing.

I must have flown my hands in a fit of rage, still clenching fists, as suddenly. A stream of bright light shone out of my right wrist and struck a mammoth skeleton, exploding the bones and sending them all over the place.

The monsters were taken aback slightly. I think to ignite the whips, I need to clench my wrists and do some sort of motion with my wrist joint. Like revving up a bike.

It worked. Two red streams burst out of my wrists like firecrackers. The rich humming of the whips was very satisfying to hear. I could see a hybrid of my blood and electric sparks in the vibrant stream.

I now had the means to strike back. I thrust my right arm with all my might like a video game character in *Mortal Kombat* towards the enemy, expecting the whip to follow swift and smite them. But no. The whip instead shot upwards towards the Whale skeletal display, striking the wires and clasps that held it up. It began to fall.

I quickly jumped out of the way, and so did Apate, but Eris was slow due to his string-like movements. The giant Whale fell on top of him in a marvellous booming display.

I heard the visual words of *boom, crash* and *snap* display all in my head.

The sound echoing throughout all of the museum like a Cherokee drum.

The entrance was free. I quickly ran for it whilst they were lost in the mayhem. Apate was pinned down. His tail trapped, but he stretched forward as fast and as far as he could and slashed my ankle. But I couldn't stop now! I quickly glanced at what remained of Barry as I ran. A tear was rolling down his dead face. I'm so sorry this had to happen to you.

Chapter 8

Like Revving an Engine

Outside, the crowds had gathered around like sheep in a flock. Pulling out their smartphones to post any kind of video on social media for their meaningless likes. My ankle was throbbing. I could feel the blood being pumped out of my body. This felt different than when the glass cut my arm. I tripped as I fell down the stairs. The concrete was hard and cold. I wanted to stay down. God knows, I just wanted to stay down and begged, prayed for this nightmare to end, but I should have known better, no God would pity me.

The monstrous howls from the Acolytes also roused me up. After all, I still had to get to my wife. The only light left in my life.

"GET UP, DANTE, THEY'LL SKEWER YOU LIKE A KEBAB!"

I struggled to get up. My muscles were roaring in pain and exhaustion. They needed rest. I needed rest.

I surveyed for a way out quick. There! In the crowd was a man on a Harley Davidson Bike. I pushed through the crowd, not caring that I knocked some of their phones out of their grasp as I barged through.

"I need your bike," I explained to the biker.

He lifted up his visor. "Piss off, bruv."

I was losing patience. "Everyone will die if I don't get out of here quick."

"Like I said, bruv, piss off!"

I felt a surge of power coursing through me, like a powerful and potent steroid.

"Get off the fucking bike or I'll kill you myself." But it wasn't my voice saying these words. It was more monstrous and demanding, like Virgil.

The biker quickly got off and backed away with his arms raised like I was pointing a gun at him. "Keys are already in," he whimpered.

I noticed his biker jacket and helmet. I would need that. My jacket was barely a jacket now anyway.

"Give me your jacket and helmet." The biker quickly complied without a word.

The jacket was snug but still bulky. A lot of padding and protection for when I'm inevitably hit or knocked over.

It was now that the crowd shifted their attention towards me. I was robbing a man after all.

"Hey, you can't do that!" one woman shouted and tried to grab my arm.

I can't help but think why are all these people up and out? Its three a.m! Go to sleep! My patience was no longer in check, as I ignited my whips to warn off the crowd. The stagnant red lights started to burn and scar the concrete pavement. They have fiery effects too it seemed. Handy.

All of us stopped in our tracks with what happened next. A resonating roar bellowed from within the museum. Now, everyone's undivided attention was directed towards the hallowed historical building. The people who still held their phones, slowly lowered them. The basic animalistic survival instinct overtook the need for internet fame. Even the cars and taxi cabs screeched to a halt. The whole city was silent as a grave. Maybe… my grave.

Large footsteps could be heard. Growing louder and louder. It was only now I snapped out of the trance and put the helmet on and lowered the visor. I revved the engine three times, ready to race out like a Formula One car.

Without a moment of build-up, the entire front section of the museum was obliterated as a large animal charged out. Flying debris was hitting everything within a mile's radius. People were crushed. Nearby buildings were damaged. The woman who tried to stop me, was impaled by a large shard of loose glass that once belonged to the massive front windows. I was miraculously unharmed by this initial bombardment. As if it were divine intervention.

The dust settled and the screams died down. I could see the beast that was our bane.

A dinosaur. More specifically, a Tyrannosaurus Rex. But it was different. Mutated. It was about fifteen metres high. Bigger than any known fossil in the species. Its skin was loose and leathery. It didn't cover the whole body, so bits of rotten flesh and skeleton bones were showing, like the ribcage and left leg. The eyes glowed a hellish red and the teeth were stained charcoal black.

It was a construct. A puppet. This was the work of Eris.

Three smaller, but still quite large, creatures followed. A triceratops, a velociraptor and a sabre-toothed tiger, whose scientific name was Smilodon, all hounded behind the alpha predator.

The triceratops was almost entirely a skeleton and stood about seven metres with yellow canine eyes.

The raptor closely resembled how they look in the movies,

but with more vibrant feathers. It had pale ghost white eyes and stood around three metres.

The Smilodon was big! About five metres. The bristly fur coat looked as if it were taken from jungle cats like leopards and tigers. The eyes were an emerald green hue.

I quickly put the bike in drive and shot off in the opposite direction. The constructs took chase and followed their prey swiftly.

I sped down the busy streets. Dodging and overtaking many cars and cabs in my haste. I was going about sixty mph. Faster than any driver has ever gone in London. Ever!

The reanimated animals were keeping up.

The traffic lights ahead at an intersection turned red. But if I stop I'm dead! But if I carry on, I'm dead! Fuck my life. No really.

A large Nisa Lorry. Probably carrying ambient food pallets to small businesses was crossing over ahead of me at the intersecting road. I was going to smash right into it! Splat like a pancake.

"DUCK!" Virgil warns me. My whole body weight shifts to the left and turns the bike handlebars right. I fell on my side with the bike resting on top of me. I was skidding off the road like James Bond! I ducked right under the chassis of the lorry! As soon as I passed it, my body kicked itself up off the tarmac with the bike, and I was back to regular old driving with two wheels firmly on the ground.

"Yes!" I shouted in amazement.

But my relief was premature. I looked behind me to make note of where my pursuers were. The zombified Triceratops rammed straight through the lorry. Obliterating it and sending chunks of destruction made of steel, wood or food products flying like shooting stars.

"Oh come on," I shouted back at them in absolute frustration.

It was now that the mega super department store Harrods was opposite me. The building was large and looked like it spanned a mile like a giant mansion. Still, it was pretty… and about to be another tourist hot spot I'll destroy.

"I HAVE AN IDEA." Just as he finishes his sentence, my body turns the handlebars and directs the bike towards one of the glass door entrances into the famous building.

Harrods had many different themed interiors decorated like an Egyptian theme, pristine white marble, a chocolate and candy hall that looked like the inside of a chocolatiers' imagination and many, many more.

As if it were destiny, I happen to bust through into the ancient Egyptian setting. Two massive statues that looked like pharaohs were on opposite sides with massive heavily ornamented escalators between them. The ceiling was decorated with images of major deities amongst the stars. I couldn't help but think they were watching me.

My right arm seized up and ignited the whip and shot it to the ceiling, anchoring it in place like a grappling hook.

"HANG ON."

I tensed my whole body as if I were petrified into place. My legs squeezing the body of the bike and my left hand still gripping the handle like my life depended on it. Which it most definitely did!

Like a bolt of lightning, I was lifted into the air at speed, still perched on the bike. I was right, Virgil used the whip as a grappling hook and boosted us up onto the highest floor above us. Like Batman! The bike landed on the shiny, faultless floor, with a crack. Oops.

"How did you know it could do that?"

"I DIDN'T."

I try not to let his lack of knowledge and careless daredevil attitude sway me, but it initially does. Until the raptor and tiger hop through the hole I just made and hiss and growl at me. I knew that a couple of elevated floors wouldn't hold them for long. So I put pedal to the metal and thrust off into the labyrinthine store.

The immediate section I was racing through must have been rich designer clothes and Gucci handbags. Stuff I could never afford.

The raptor was the most immediate threat. It hopped over mannequins and displays of shoes and hand wear to try to cut me off and ponce on me. It was fast. Faster than I was going in these cramped linear halls.

I ignited my left whip. The raptor was closing in. Closer. Closer. It snapped its jaws trying to bite a chunk out of me. I swerved right and with a fancy flick of my wrist, the whip shot out and sliced the raptor's head off with a flash and bang.

Its body flopped straight to the floor and began to shrink back to a skeleton and its regular size. The reanimated flesh singed off and machinery, rock and preserved fish specimens flopped out of its once again hollow ribcage. Those must have been what Eris used to create his monstrous puppets.

But now I have one thought. Where is that tiger?

It was now that the sprinklers were set off. The smoke from my whip now emitting and radiating off the scorch marks. But this light rain would be no help for what comes next...

The tyrannosaur busted its giant head through the exterior brick wall. Its large head narrowly missing me. I was on the fourth floor, just to exaggerate its sheer height to reach me like this. Thankfully it's too big and fat to come inside. But Eris concocted a hidden weapon inside the monster's gullet. It opened its jaws wide. I could see gears turning and clicking. And a spark. Flames began to shoot out and completely envelop everything it touched. The sound it made was terrifying. A cross between a cheetah hiss and a woman's deafening scream. I turned the bike in the other direction and shot off like a bat out of hell. All the water from the sprinklers evaporated in an instant. The priceless hours of work and effort that went into the majesty of Harrods was gone in an instant. Burning.

Ahead was a window. My way out. Until a flurry of flames crossed me off. I turned left to avoid the fiery wall. The heat was intense. I felt like a microwave meal, and the timer was almost up. Tick, tock.

But fate would deny me this burning end. Ahead was another window. This was my last chance. The flames had me walled in like a trench run. This was it. Do or die…

I crash through the window, splitting through glass and wind, descending into the street below. Behind me I could feel the deadly embrace of fire. Flames busted through every crack, crevice and window of Harrods building. Ultimately leading to what felt like a nuclear explosion. The whole building, poof. I land with solemn thoughts. How much unwanted pain and chaos can one bring before the sun even rises? When I learnt that I was the saviour of mankind, I didn't picture this. London is a warzone.

I just hope that tiger creature is burning inside. It isn't. The tiger leaps out of the inferno and lands on top of a car. Crushing it and anyone inside. Its skin was smouldering off like ice cream on a hot summer's day.

Remember, it's not alive. It's not alive. Feel no sympathy. It will show no such compassion to me. It roars. I roar back. Rev, rev. The purring engine of the bike roars too.

With a wheel spin and some dirty tire marks, I'm off once more into the night.

I hear what sounds like radio frequencies in my head. Like trying to tune into the correct station. Some voices fall into concentration.

"The Slayer is involved. Repeat. The Slayer is involved."

"Copy that, hunter one. Drones are deployed"

Clover. I can hear any messages they send out or receive now that I've absorbed their radio frequencies. And now, not only do I have to deal with the reanimated past, but high tech drones are after me. What a perfectly normal life you lead, Dante Adler.

"Drones, Virgil?" I shout over the hustling noise of beeping cars and roaring animals.

"DO NOT PANIC. THIS COULD PROVE FRUITFUL."

"How?"

"THE DRONES MUST BE FILLED WITH ANTI-GOD WEAPONRY. MORE THAN ENOUGH FIREPOWER TO PUT DOWN A REANIMATED CAT."

The whizzing noise of drone propellers was getting louder and closer. They soon reached eye contact. They were black, bulky and resembled Manta Rays with machine guns loaded underneath. The barrels began to spin, powering them up. Green bullets shot out like paint gun pellets. Everything they hit seemed to melt with a green and yellow flash. Note to self: don't get hit.

Fortunately, age has not made the sabre-toothed tiger any wiser. A bombardment of bullets penetrates its exposed flesh and bone reducing it to acidic slime.

Two down. Two to go. Three horns and Rexy.

The next moments were silent. Eerily silent. No cars. No people. Not even some of Clover's drones. Everybody had just disappeared, just like the train station. As if survival instincts had made them all go to bed. I hear a snort, like it had just been blown out of a cow's wet nose. I put the brakes on and watch, a large figure is standing in front of me about a block away.

The triceratops was still. The only movement was the scraping of its front left foot against the road, like a bull about to charge. I rev the engine three times in response. Accepting the challenge, three horns roars and charges. Its footsteps rumbled the ground like a mini earthquake. The parked cars hopped in the air with their alarms set off as it zoomed past. I set off with a wheelie. Ready to attack. We were getting closer to one another. Closer. Closer. With thunderbolt reflexes, I perform the same trick as I did to avoid the Nisa truck. I slide under the beast. My right whip ignites and I flick the red stream up.

Slice.

The dinosaur stops. Stunned with disbelief in its tracks. A crack splits down the middle of its skull and spreads over the spine and under the belly culminating by reaching the tail.

Split.

One half falls right. The other, to the left. Need I say more?

Without a moment's reprieve, I'm struck from the bike and sent flying. I land not too far from the dead again Trike.

It was the Rex. It whipped me with its tail and was standing proudly from doing the deed. The equivalent of a smug face for a dinosaur was struck across its brow.

My vision began to blur. Something was wrong. This wasn't from the tail whip. This was something else. Worse. Darker.

I could barely hear Virgil trying to talk to me, but the transmission was fuzzy and obscured.

Behind me was a park with lots of trees and bushes. I needed to use them for cover. I ran like a panicked and wounded animal into the wood.

No light came in here. The shroud of shadows from the twisted trees was enough. It looked way more sinister and malformed than from the outside, like the woods decided to be redesigned by Tim Burton.

I hid under a pile of fallen leaves. The pounding and booming footsteps grew closer. Even the water in the puddles was rippling, just like in the movies.

Boom!

It was standing right next to my cover.

Sniff. Sniff.

I didn't need super human senses to know it was lowering its head down to the pile of leaves I was hiding in. I thought for sure, this was the end.

Bang! Bang!

The Tyrannosaur reared up and roared at the drones that had just shot at it. Now was my chance to escape. I stood up and ran, but then a voice came into my head. Mine.

Don't run, fight. Fight! Fight!

Slay.

I snapped back to reality and turned to face my foe. It had just finished ripping apart the last of the attack drones. It stared straight at me. Into my very soul. Its eyes blazed hellfire and erupted its flaming breath from its throat. I quickly leaped into the trees to evade the sea of fire. Luckily the twisted bodies of bark made it easy to hop from tree to tree, evading the dreaded jaws of death.

Snap! Snap!

But it could not catch me. I climb to the tallest tree I can. Even higher than the Rex at full height. I have a plan.

The Rex raises its head, about to unleash its fires again. I jump. Ignite. And fling a whip straight down its gullet into the machine that powers its inferno.

I land in a superhero pose. The Rex freezes. Smoke billows from any escape it can. A chain reaction begins blowing up the dinosaur from the inside out. I knew that attacking its combustion engine would be its bane.

It falls and begins to disintegrate, just like the others, in defeat. I win.

As I wander back to the gleaming lights of civilisation, I feel a sting in my heart. I grip my chest and fall to my knees. My vision blurred again. I spat out drops of erratic blood. The cut on my ankle was heating up. The wound was oozing black liquid like a filled up, overflowing drain, similar to what these Acolytes are drenched in.

"POISON." I could hear Virgil's words again. And he didn't have anything good to say. "POISON, DANTE. WE'VE BEEN POISONED!"

Chapter 9

Wounded

I am the luckiest, unluckiest man in the world. Perhaps history. If this pain kicked in whilst I was fighting the cast of Jurassic Park, I'd be extinct too.

"I thought you could heal me?"

Virgil speaks with a hint of urgency and panic, "I CAN HEAL MORTAL WOUNDS, LIKE CUTS AND BLACK EYES. BUT THIS, IS A GODLY WOUND. THE POISON BLADE OF APATE IS POTENT AND POWERFUL. EXTRACTED FROM A DEAD ROOT OF YGGDRASILL. THE WORLD TREE."

I need to get to a hospital. I need help. I perch on the bike seat and painfully twist the ignition keys. That was so much harder than it should be. I take off the helmet. The darkened view through the visor was making things worse, (safety be dammed). Believe it or not, I made it about two hundred metres going slow, about fifteen mph before I fell off through exhaustion and dizziness. The bike was of no use to me at this moment now. There's no way I could stabilise myself on it. It would feel like drink driving and being high on cocaine at the same time. Not that I would know what that combo feels like.

I wander through back alleys, stumbling over garbage bins and scurrying rats. The ground was wet with rain and leaking wet waste. Trying to find a pharmacy or anything that could stimulate me to keep on going.

A shifty looking man wearing dark grey clothing and a beanie introduced himself. He was holding pornographic magazines, but opened them up revealing small plastic bags filled with different coloured powders and pills.

"Hey man, want some drugs?"

Although a pill of something illegal would no doubt boost me, I say nothing and keep on walking/stumbling. Don't want to add drug addict to my CV.

"It's good stuff, man. I saw dinos walking about, man, like its Jurassic something, man. It's a good batch." I must have been out of his eye line now and he was still shouting, trying to sell me stuff. "If you change your mind, man, my name's Guy. I'll be making my way towards London Bridge if you want a slice, man."

I get the feeling that I'll be seeing him again. Knowing my luck.

Just like the three wise men from the Nativity, I find my holy star saviour. A bright sign saying 'Miss Marzipan's Veterinary Clinic for animals' gleams before me. I guess a vets are better than nothing.

It was a small corner shop that looked very friendly and inviting to those in distress. The windows were decorated with displays of dog medication, animal harnesses for support whilst walking and cat toothpastes.

The back door was easy to open. I still had a slither of super strength. There was no alarm siren. Meaning it would definitely be a silent alarm. There is no way that 'Miss Marzipan' would leave this place without any security. I'd have to be quick.

The storage room was filled with all types of unpleasant medicines. Digestion pastes for horses and liver cleansing tablets were the most discouraging of the lot.

"Any ideas, Virgil?"

"TRY THE XL WORMER TABLETS. THE PRAZIQUENTEL SHOULD PREVENT THE POISON FROM GETTING THICKER IN THE STOMACH. THE POISON IS SUPPOSED TO TARGET HERE AND CAUSE A CHAIN REACTION, FORCING YOU TO THROW UP YOUR INTERNAL ORGANS."

How charming. I pop off the cap of the bottle. Bottoms up. They taste like wet socks found in a toilet bowl.

"NOW GO TO THE SURGERY."

The surgery was clean and stainless after I switched on the lights. Not one drop of evidence that it had ever been used. The staff really take care of this place.

"TAKE THAT GAS CANISTER"

A lone canister was left next to the operating table with a nozzle and a small plastic face mask at the end of it. I turn the can to look at the label, 'Flutothane'. It was an anaesthetic gas.

"What's this for?"

"INHALING."

"Funny. How do you turn it on?"

"PROBABLY THE LITTLE VALVE AT THE TOP."

I reach for it, but my other hand smacks it away like an old granny when her grandkid tries to take a piece of chocolate cake. "NOT YET," he spites. "WE NEED THOSE." My arm flings forward pointing at the defibrillators, in the corner.

"You can't be serious? What are you gonna do, stop my heart?"

An awkward silence rings louder than any word he has ever said.

"YES."

"Fucking why?"

"DON'T WORRY, PRINCESS. I'M GONNA KICKSTART YOUR HEART WITH THOSE THINGS."

"Let me just rewind a bit if I wasn't being clear. Fucking why?"

Virgil shushes me. I did lose my temper a bit. "IT WILL TRICK THE POISON INTO THINKING YOU'RE DEAD, AND THEREFORE CEASE TO SPREAD… TEMPORARILY."

"Temporarily?"

"YOU REALLY THINK THE REMEDY FOR WORLD TREE POISON WILL BE FOUND IN A VET?"

"…No."

"DIDN'T THINK SO. NOW BRING THE DEFIBRILLATORS AND LIE DOWN."

I prepare the small operating table and take off my (stolen) jacket and shirt. It was cold and nippy. The small plastic face mask for the gas was obviously for dogs or cats, so was awkward to put on. The defibrillators were charged to maximum voltage. The needle was in the red 'danger' area. The gas was primed. Everything was ready. Now I just have to die.

"Promise me, you'll bring me back," I shakily say.

"I PROMISE."

I leave the controls of my body to Virgil and try to relax. My right arm raises to turn the nozzle of the Flutothane canister. It made a slight squeaking noise as it spun. The vapour poured in. It smelt of strawberries. My eyelids began to flicker. My vision grows black. My eyes shut. Then nothing. Infinite, nothingness.

"Aaaaaahhhh!" I scream in pain as I'm jolted awake and fall off the silver reflective table. My heart is pounding like a jackhammer about to burst out of my chest. I take the stupid and small face covering off and try to catch my breath. A bit of spew comes up and I spit it all on the floor like green yellow paint. I think I can see my bagel from lunch.

"Oh God!" I clasp my hands over my face.

"WELCOME BACK TO THE LAND OF THE LIVING!"

"Shut your fucking mouth," I exasperatingly say back.

After a while, I catch my breath back. "How long was I gone?"

"I don't know," a strange woman's voice comments.

I quickly spring up and turn to this new face. A woman in her late twenties, probably a little older than me, was standing with her arms crossed. She wore a dark green army jacket and cargo pants. Her blonde hair was tucked behind her ears.

"By the time I got here it looked like you were trying to defibrillate yourself. That was twenty minutes ago. I helped you."

"Thank you. Miss Marzipan, I presume?" That was all I could think to ask.

"She was my mum. It's Mrs by the way, thank you very much."

"Sorry." I grab my shirt and slip it back on. "I can explain."

"Really? Because what it looks like is that some junkie broke into my family business and tried to perform some sort of auto erotic asphyxiation whilst high on dog wormer and flutothane gas!"

As I slip my (stolen) biker's jacket back on, I ask "I would've thought you'd have called the police or ambulance by now then. Some stranger in your shop."

"You don't know? Whole City is on fire. Emergency Services are all on call."

Unfortunately, I do know, but she doesn't need to know that. "Jeez," I say.

"Yep." She pauses and glances down at my ankle. "Your ankle was pretty messed up. What'd you take?"

I nervously look around. "Bad… stuff."

"Bad stuff?"

"BAD STUFF?"

After a brief pause, contemplating my poor choice of words. "Yeah," I finally speak. "Look. I'm not here to hurt you or mess anything here up. I've done what I came here to do. Thank you for helping me."

"The news is looking for someone by the way. A man in black."

The Man in Black. That's what Barry and a lot of internet personalities called me. It must have caught on.

"You want to know my story, former Ms Marzipan? I'm a very special kind of exterminator. The things that treat the human race like play things. Causing violence, wars, disease and famine, all for fucking laughs or vain agendas. That's what I kill. Gods and their monsters. Yeah I'm the Man in Black. But my true title is a Godslayer. I'm the only reason the World is not ruled by a single deity fascist and their cults."

The lady says nothing. She lowers her arms. She looks like she is processing this information. "Why were you here?"

I exasperate a puff of air and raise my trouser to show my ankle. "I was poisoned by a thing called 'Apate'. The stuff here can keep me alive for a bit longer. But it's not permanent."

"What is it? Apate I mean."

Does this lady actually believe me? "I'm not sure. I have, like… a kind of wisdom in my head, that guides me. Tells me what to do. Keeps me alive. I know it's an Acolyte of Death."

The lady walks into what I think is her office. She comes back with a bottle of Evian Water.

“My name’s Izzy,” She says with a smile

I feel so warm inside. I had won her trust after a five-minute conversation.

“Why are you helping me?” I ask as I take the plastic bottle.

“You’ve changed the world. Godslayer. Besides haven’t you noticed?” She points to the door to the kennel area. “The animals that stay here overnight have not made a single bark, growl or hiss. They sense the pureness in you.”

She was right. I never even thought about the animals here. Not one hiss from a snake, or squeak from a gerbil. That stabilises my unsteady soul, and makes me want to cry with contempt.

“Thank you, Izzy. My name is Dante by the way.”

We shake hands. Mutual respect is known between us. I make my way back out…

“Um, Izzy?”

“Yeah?”

“Please don’t tell anyone you saw me. There’s also this shady organisation after me.”

Izzy imitates zipping her mouth shut. I smile back and make my exit through the back door.

The sun was rising on a new day. On a new world. There was a slight hint of mist pouring over the city like a blanket of vapour. The streets were still barren and empty. No doubt that everyone was glued to their TV screens watching the morning news. Trying to make sense of the many strange events that befell Surrey last night. Izzy the vet was right; I had changed the way the world works. But there was one developing story I couldn’t shake out of my head…

“You failed to bring me back!” I shout at Virgil. Not caring if I wake anyone who might still be sleeping in a twenty-mile radius.

"NOT TRUE. I WAS NEARLY THERE WHEN IZZY WALKED IN."

"How long was I really out?"

Silence.

"thirty-two MINUTES AND twenty-five SECONDS."

"Idiot." I clap back. My voice turns solemn with my next question, "What were they, Virgil? All you've said is that they were Acolytes of Death."

"ITS COMPLICATED. DEATH IS A CONSTANT. A SORT OF METAPHYSICAL BEING. NOT PHYSICAL OR CORPOREAL IN THIS KNOWN WORLD. BUT IT EXISTS BETWEEN THE KNOWN AND UNKNOWN. THE ACOLYTES ARE RELIGIOUS DEVOTEES AND CONCUBINES TO THIS FORCE. THEY WILL DO ANYTHING TO PLEASE THEIR INVISIBLE MASTER. THERE ARE SEVEN—"

"Like the Seven Deadly Sins?" I cut in.

"NO," he continues, "THE SINS ARE FAR MORE DEADLY AND POWERFUL. IF THE SKY FATHERS SENT THEM TO KILL US. WE WOULD NOT BE ALIVE."

"Then why didn't they?"

"WOULD AN ARMY SEND A BATTLESHIP TO SQUASH AN ANT?"

He has a fair point. Touché. "No. I guess not."

"EXACTLY. THE SEVEN ACOLYTES ARE AVATARS REPRESENTING DIFFERENT KINDS OF TORTURE."

He tells me about the avatars and their names.

Geras. Old age. The one that I called 'The Bride in Black'. That was her.

Apate. Deception. One of the things from the museum. The

Blade Snake.

Eris. Strife. The puppet who brought the fossils back to life.

Oizys. Suffering.

Moros. Doom.

Momus. Blame.

Nemesis. Retribution.

The last four I haven't had the pleasure of meeting yet. But I'm sure I will soon enough. Virgil also says that they are like rabid dogs that need to be on a leash. The Gods wouldn't let them loose without someone who controls them, and that I should look out for whomever holds their whip!

Chapter 10

Saint Esta Hospital

You probably don't know the story of Saint Esta. It's not a very widespread tale. I didn't know too until Virgil told me.

It's about a French woman in the fourteenth century, accused of witchcraft and black magic. Though the tale tells that she was a healer, soothsayer and prophet who never even hurt a fly.

She resided in a small hut just outside of Paris. She grew herbs and flowers in her little garden by the river.

Families would bring their sick relatives to be healed by her magic touch, and it always worked. Children would grow to be brave knights. The elderly would live for a decade longer. The sick would get a spring in their step. It was magic.

Esta too read palms and predicted futures for those who pay. She predicted the harvest, the winds and the river.

A hunter, named Ren, grew infatuated with her, and soon, so too did she. They were in love. A fairy-tale kind of love. Pure, sweet and innocent.

She was loved by most. Not all.

You see, when people don't understand something, they get violent, aggressive and seek to destroy it. A small group of Christian zealots took her from her home. On her wedding day. She was gowned in white silk that the spiders had weaved for her. She was burnt at the stake, and the crispy body was thrown into the Seine river.

Over history though, thankfully, Esta's good deeds were remembered and preserved. She was named an honorary Saint, and the Royal London hospital was renamed after her in her honour, when it reopened in 2012.

That's my next destination. Tower Hamlets. Whitechapel.

The new building was big and bulky, like blue and white Lego blocks had been stacked together with cube boxes in between them for structure and support.

The queues were chaotic outside. It must have been a mile long with people in stretchers or wheelchairs. Parents clasping their babes and children tightly in their arms.

Burn victims. Wounded elders. Frightened people. This one woman, kept repeating the same word, over and over, kissing the Christian cross she had on her necklace between breaths.

"Monsters. Monsters. Monsters."

Inside, the chaos was still prevalent, just in a more condensed space.

Doctors rushing patients to any operating space they could find.

"Excuse me," I ask the receptionist. "Mia Adler? I'm her husband."

"Room 204," the receptionist quickly says. She was also on the phone, telling people they have no space to spare.

Mia was sleeping when I entered. She looked healthy. No blood pouring anywhere. Her breathing was soft. It was quieter in here, but I could still hear the hustle and bustle outside the doors a bit. I sit on the chair by the bedside and take Mia's hand in my own.

The noise drowns quieter and quieter… But I know this trick now…

“I used to help people,” A broken voice sounds from the dark corner of the room. “They punished me for that.” It was a woman’s tone, she sounded as if she were crying.

I let go of my wife’s hand and stand to face the enemy. I’m not afraid.

“I was going to be a wife once. They punished me for that.” The figure exited the shadows. It was Geras, avatar of suffering. The Bride in Black. But I deduced who she really was now…

“Esta,” I say with sympathy.

The bride twisted and cracked as she moved. Her dress was tattered and ripped.

“Esta. Yes. I think my mother used to call me that,” she says with a hint of wonder in her dead eyes. “Sweet Esta. Lovely sweet Esta. So warm.”

Esta was a true corpse. Her body looked as if it had been rotting for over five hundred years. Which of course it had been.

“I’m sorry for what happened to you, Esta.”

“Esta is dead.” She snaps like a twig. “I am Geras.”

“Geras is older than you Esta. You’re a woman from Paris. Geras is a figure from ancient Greece.”

Esta stumbles, but catches herself on the wall, before she falls. “Endless time. Like a river. I could not die, as the water crushed me. I sought sanctuary, from any power. That’s when he found me. Brought me into the family.”

“Who, Esta? Who controls the Acolytes?”

“The Ferryman,” she shrieks as she tries to hide in a dark corner, as if she is afraid to speak the name. “Those who seek to find a way out, do not, but scream and shout. For if he deems you worthy and true, it’s off to see the Ferryman for you…” she rhymes in her corner.

Esta screams and disappears once more as a band of orange

chains tendril around her again. I'm left with few answers and more questions. I know that the Acolytes change over the years with new hosts. It seems this 'Ferryman', is the leader and chooses them to join the 'family'. Is he the one who is hunting me? The one who holds the whip?

"I'm sorry about your wife." Another strange woman enters the fray.

"I'm thinking that maybe I should try to grow some eyes in the back of my head." I turn to face the woman, expecting another hideous creature, but no. She was a fair woman, who didn't look the least bit threatening. I recognised her though, from movies. Evie Star. What is she doing here?

Evie walks over and places her palm on Mia's forehead, "She'll be fine."

"I know who you are. Evie Star… I just don't know *what* you are," I threaten.

Evie smirks. "There's no fooling you now, is there Godslayer? You've seen so much in just a few hours." She gets uncomfortably close to my face, examining it. "Yes. I see the change has begun. Your eyes are nearly yellow. The area around your eyes is turning black like makeup. Your bloodlust replacing your human emotions. It's all standard."

Yellow? Last time I checked my eyes were blue. I briefly thought they might have been looking green, but I assumed that was just the light, and what's this about having biological eye shadow?

"What are you?" I grab her and slam her against the wall. Evie grabs me by the wrists and starts to bend them backwards. She is far stronger than I.

"Temper, temper." She lets go finally. "Why I'm of course Evie Star, award winning actor and number one on Vogue's most inspirational women. But I also go by Brunhilda."

I recognise that name. Brunhilda. A warrior angel known as a Valkyrie. They're supposed to guide souls to Valhalla in Norse mythology.

"Oh, sorry about poor Esta slipping through my fingers again, so sorry."

It's her! She is the one who controls them! The one who's hunting me.

"How are you controlling them?"

"A magician should never reveal her trick." She pops a strange looking stone with a rune carved on it back into her pocket.

"So you're who Daddy Zeus sent to kill me? Well do it!" I shout back in defiance.

"That is what the council ordered me to do, but I have a proposition." My ears prick up. "It concerns you, and her." She points to Mia with intent.

"What?"

"Questions, questions, questions. That is all you ever ask." She picks me up and sets me down on the bedside chair. Evie, then snaps her fingers, and a chair of mist appears as she slowly sits. The disguised Valkyrie begins a speech.

"Yes, I am the one sent here to kill you. Yes, I am the one who is 'supposed' to control the Acolytes for this job, but they are very sneaky, and look at the damage they've caused!" She puts her hand on her chest. "For that I am truly sorry." I can't tell if she is being serious or sarcastic. "But… I don't want to kill you. That brings me to my proposition. Give me the girl, and I can hide you from the White City forever. By Helheim, you can even come join us!"

I don't believe what I'm hearing. I feel angry butterflies in my stomach churning and fluttering. They want my wife? For what sinister reason? My fists clench so hard I could cut into them with my nails.

"Why?" I grit through my teeth.

"Your wife is the last living heir to Pandora."

The revelation hits me like a bulldozer. The air itself turns stale like Barley. The anger, like drunken rage.

"How are you sure?"

"Poor Mia there is the only other survivor of the Devil's Little Sinners incident. The other being you of course. I had my suspicions. So I did a little research in the Halls of Knowledge. Turns out she is the last heir."

"What about her parents. They are both still alive."

Evie's smile widens. "You don't know? Mia is adopted."

The puzzle was coming together. Both Virgil and I shared suspicions about Mia's lack of injury compared to the others, but we didn't discuss it further at the time.

Evie sniffs the air. "It turns out Clover are nearly here." I hurry to the window to look outside. Sure enough four black SUVs pulled up outside. Led by Agents Tom Grayson and Harry Lyle. Evie continues, "My covenant has use for her and by gracious extension, you. You have till the Hallowed Solstice at midnight to make up your mind. I promise no Acolytes shall interfere until then. Goodbye."

And with that, both Evie and the chair vanished into a hiss of green mist.

Hallowed Solstice? There's something else to google and worry about. It's no coincidence, it's Halloween tomorrow. But now I have to get her out of here. I try to shake 'Sleeping Beauty' awake, but no such luck, she was still drugged.

Luckily, the bed could be wheeled off, like when transporting a patient for surgery. A gurney. I pushed her out into the corridor. Sure I got some worried and discombobulated looks from staff, but I have more pressing matters to concern me.

Gotta think, gotta think, I keep repeating to myself as I push her into the elevator and push the button down to ground floor.

I could just stroll down London, pushing a hospital patient through Covent Garden? No that's stupid.

Steal an ambulance? Good enough.

The elevator doors open. Tom and Harry are standing right there and caught off guard. Tom spots me and orders his men to stop me. I kick him in the groin as he tries to grab me.

I hastily press the 'close doors' button. Agent Harry, however, was as nimble as a ninja and managed to weasel his way into the elevator and wrestle with me.

Amidst the struggle, one of our butts must have hit an elevator button, as we soon rose up to the fifth floor. We both fall out, wriggling on the floor, when the doors shift open. Harry soon gets the upper hand and gets on top. His hands feel different, laced with some sort of sedative for Gods and other beings. That's why he's getting the upper hand.

"Your kind make me sick!" He spits in my face.

A sprinkle of dust falls on top of us, followed by small slices and chunks of debris from the ceiling. Harry looks up in distress. A large golden arm smashes through and grabs Harry's head and pulls him up into the hole, disappearing.

I recognise that arm though…

A large figure smashes through the ceiling behind me. The dust clears and I see my oldest foe.

Herakles stood before me. He was larger and more golden than before. More wild and bestial, like a gorilla. His body could barely fit in this hospital hallway. His sword was still sheathed in a scabbard on his back, but now it looks as if he could hold it in one hand. He held Harry in his arm, who was still screaming. Herakles grasped the agent's head with his other hand and ripped it clean off like a plaster. The crimson liquid sprayed these once white halls red. He lifted the decapitated body to his mouth and began drinking straight from the fresh source.

He threw the drained body away like a discarded toy when he had his fill of blood. The head, he squashed like jelly under his titanic foot.

He raised his eyes to meet mine. This was personal to him.

"Ready for round two, little princess?"

Chapter 11

All You Can Eat Buffet

The beast pounded its chest with its fists, challenging me, one on one.

"You'll pay for damaging my sacred body," he snarled.

Despite his intent to use my skull as a literal toilet bowl, I feel no animosity or hatred towards him, now that I know the truth about his story. I feel only sympathy.

"We don't need to fight, Herakles." I try to reason with him. "This monster you've become is not your fault. It is your father's."

Snort. I get no cognitive reply from the former man.

"I also know of the spear." Herakles' eyes open wide. "And the old man on the mountain."

The animal charges at me before I can say another word. The whips blaze on in my wrists. He swings his giant arm to hit me, but I've learnt a lot since the night before. I jump over the tree trunk sized arm with grace and lash him over the face with a whip.

He retreats slightly back. "The Blood Whips of Pompeii," he whispers to himself. "You've armed yourself, princess. I've got a few tricks as well."

The muscles on his body begin to ripple like water. They contract and expand. His bones pop out like they're about to tear through his skin. His teeth became too big for his mouth and hung out slightly like tusks. He was growing bigger. The hair on his arms grew longer. The skin, now a pure gold colour.

The floor beneath us could no longer support our weight. It cracked and gave way.

The battle raged on however. Luckily, the sheer size of his gargantuan body, meant that he could no longer keep himself upright. Due in part to the limited space in a standard room, and because his spine could not support his gargantuan weight. He was slower than usual, but still mighty fast.

"MIGHT I SUGGEST A TACTICAL RETREAT," the inner voice chimes in after taking a break.

"You mean run away? Where have you been anyway?"

But no reply. Virgil was acting off. Nevertheless, maybe a 'tactical retreat' would be beneficial.

I run through the maze that was the hospital. Making quick turns left and right, and then left again, trying to create some space between me and the raging gorilla.

I shout at whomever can hear or move to "Quickly get out of the building!" whilst also trying to avoid the most crowded areas.

I take the stairs up to the twelfth floor. Oncology. AKA the cancer ward. Running up those stairs was really hard. I try to catch my breath back. I think I have a stitch as well…

A roar bellowed from underneath the floor. The pounding, *boom! Boom! Boom!* Grew louder.

Herakles busted through as if it were made of paper, and snarled at me.

"I've… got… your scent… Dante." He sounds out of breath. He looks slightly paler as well. More yellow than actual gold. I'm not even concerned that he now knows me by name. He wheezes,

"Need… food." He turns his back and slugs his way towards a patient room. I can't let him eat any more people!

I rush into the ward and find him lumbering over a poor patient, sick due to the chemotherapy, crying with fear. I try to help, but Herakles smacks me away with the back of his hand.

"Forgive… me," he whimpers as he lowers his jaws for a bite of the patient's arm.

Chomp!

What follows is a scream, but not from the bedridden patient. The low rumbling squeal of the giant is what my ears hear.

"Burns… It burns." What follows is a slew of blood being coughed from his throat.

Herakles, in a panic, tries to escape through the hall he came in through, but I ensnare him with the whips.

If I put two and two together now… the chemo! The cancer cells! He can't consume what's being killed as it grows, and it seems the bigger he gets, the more he needs to consume to sustain it. Chemo kills living cells. Added with the unfortunate circumstance of cancer, they must not agree with a Demi God's stomach.

Herakles breaks the entanglement and makes his escape with haste. I need to act fast. Stop him from eating anyone else and make him drink his medicine.

A slight shuffling occurs behind me in the debris. A doctor makes her presence known.

"Is it over?" She shrivels.

I help her back to her feet. "Listen Doctor…" I look at her name tag. "Clifton. I need packets of chemotherapy solution. Or vials of cancer patients' blood. They're the only things that can stop him."

She collects herself and tells me to follow her. She leads me to a small lab for tests and storage. She hands me three packets of the solution and five vials of blood.

"Kill that son of a bitch!" she asks me.

"I'm not trying to kill him. I'm going to try and cure him." I swiftly exit back into the hallway and jump down through the giant hole in the ground.

It was easy to find him. Just follow the screams. There were handprints located all along the ground, walls and ceiling, where he had been dragging himself along. Lights were flickering on and off, like a run-down asylum.

"Herakles!" I shout as I turn the corner, facing the behemoth. He was slowing down. "Got your medicine." I shake the bags and vials. He growls.

We charge at each other, ending in a collision that sends visible shockwaves. He pins me down and starts snapping his jaws like a crocodile, inching closer and closer towards my face. But I keep him back, and between snaps, lodge a bag of chemo between his sharp teeth. Pop.

"It burns!" he shouts in anguish. Trying to rub the solution off his tongue.

In his panic, I quickly throw two vials of the blood down his throat. I felt horrible doing this to him, but my hypothesis was working. He began to shrink and turn paler still.

Herakles bounded out of the nearest wall that led to the outside in retreat. He landed amongst the queue of waiting patients outside and roared at them to flee.

"Need... Pure... Food." I could hear him chanting to himself.

He could now stand upright, not restricted to limited space thanks to his shrunken size, but he was still dangerous and on the hunt.

I anchored a whip into the side of the building and repelled down SAS style to the ground. Then retracted it back like a measuring tape.

"I know what the Gods have done to you." I try to reassure him. "They're using you for sport. You're a pawn to them."

"Shut up!" He grabs a parked car and chucks it at me. Luckily, no one was inside. I flip over, the car does not hit anyone thankfully. As I'm in the air, I throw a bag straight into his eyes.

"Argh, my eyes!" He clutches his face and begins to shake.

"It was Hera, who turned you into this. Zeus who allowed it to happen. He made you do those labours, never to welcome you to Olympus, but to make fun of you!"

"Stop!"

"He banished you for lack of restraint. From Zeus, who fucks anything that breathes! Hypocrite!" I grasp one of the vials in my right hand and jump to meet his face and sucker punch him in the mouth. Forcing him to have to swallow the blood.

"Stop it!" he begs me.

"You saved Greece from slavery. Perhaps even helped preserve Western Civilisation! You were a hero!" Herakles was weakening, his golden hue almost completely gone. I whip him, bringing him to his knees. I grasp him by the throat and shove the last packet down his throat. He was too weak to even attempt to bite my arm off.

"Please..."

"They used you! Made you a monster!" I place the last of the vials in his mouth and punch him in the throat, forcing him to swallow glass and blood. Herakles was now his original size. Only about above average height. His muscles reduced to nothing. He was as pale as a ghost and as skinny as an anorexia sufferer. His hair was thin and wispy. He was no threat now.

He shrivelled into the foetal position. Trying to rub himself warm.

"So… cold."

I picked him up like a damsel in distress. I turned to find the whole crowd watching me with eager eyes. Waiting to see what I'd do next.

I leave the crowd and whip my way up to the top roof of the building and lay my foe on the ground and grasp his hand in respect.

"I've done terrible things… for people I've never known. I've held onto false hope for so long," he whispers. A tear rolling down his frail cheek.

"Everyone does. We've all made mistakes. It's what makes us human."

"But… we are not just human." He pants.

"No, that's true. But it's that part of us that is strongest. The part with determination, sympathy… and love."

Herakles rolls his weak head to look at me. "Do you think my family… would still love me… if I joined them in Elysium?"

"I don't know. But honour your family. By helping me save mine."

Herakles closes his eyes, and drifts off to a deep rest. Without giving an answer.

Chapter 12

Gungarok

I left the cold body on the roof. I tried to check if he were still alive, but I guess the ol' pulse check on the neck or on the wrists doesn't translate well to Demi God biology, as I couldn't detect any trace of a heartbeat on him. I guess Herakles, the son of Zeus, is now dead.

Back on the ground, pandemonium kicked in. The people didn't know what to do. To cheer. To panic. To clap, or even pray.

The news vans arrived by now, with reporters in cheap suits that were made to look expensive, jumping out of the sliding doors with minimum wage cameramen following. Now was the time for me to leave.

I found Mia being tended to by a paramedic on the bottom floor. She had woken up.

"Mia." I give her a hug. "Are you okay?"

"Yeah, I'm doing fine. What is going on though?" The paramedic gives me a look of deception when she asks me this.

"All your questions will be answered, but now, we need to go."

"Um, sir," the paramedic tells me, "This woman needs medical attention. She's not going anywhere."

"I appreciate your concern, but she will be fine. Trust me," I tell her.

"But sir…"

"You've seen what I can do. Haven't you?" I threaten the paramedic. Mia looks at me with an expression I've never seen before. Disgust.

I pick Mia up and make my way to a parked ambulance and load Mia into the back.

"What the fuck are you doing? Dante!" she screams at me as I close the back doors on her.

I can see people gossiping, pulling out their phones and attempting to ring the police. The Clover agents exit the hospital, looking for me.

I get into the driver's seat of the ambulance. No keys. Fuck.

A small stream of whip is ignited in my right hand and the light slips into the ignition slot. The purring engine shocks to life.

"Thanks, Virgil, didn't know they could do that." But Virgil has no witty remark, insult or wisdom to depart. Again.

Later, on the road, I give Mia the answers;

"The Gods from all mythology are hunting us. Specifically, Brunhilda, but she's actually Hollywood actress Evie Star. She is using these things called the Acolytes of Death as her personal hounds. They are what attacked us at the club and destroyed the Natural History Museum… and Harrods."

"You blew up Harrods!"

"No. I was there, but I didn't blow it up. There were these dinosaurs that were brought back to life by one of the Acolytes. They are the ones who blew up Harrods."

"…Clyde and Regina?" I give a sombre look in the rear-view mirror. She understands the language my eyes are speaking.

"The guy at the Hospital was Herakles," I add.

"Hercules?"

"No. Well yes. His real name is Herakles. A group of Romans mispronounced it and it became common knowledge after that. He took revenge by eating them."

"Why are they after us? And what's happened to your face?" she asks.

"I'm the Godslayer. The only semi-mortal being that is a threat to them. I have another voice in my head, whom I've called Virgil. He's like the collective knowledge of my past incarnations. But he's being quiet at the moment… And the more symbiotic we become… the more my appearance changes for some reason. Brunhilda mentioned something about bloodlust."

"And what about me?" she asks quietly.

I was about to tell her, but hesitated at the last second. The tyres suddenly give way and explode. I struggle to gain control of the out-of-control vehicle, but am soon able to stop it in its tracks with some hard steering and braking.

"Are you okay?" I shout back.

"Nothing a few years of therapy won't fix."

There was a knock on the driver seat window. Upon inspection, I recognised the face of the individual who knocked on the glass.

Guy the drug dealer was standing with a smile on his face, still holding his pornographic magazines firmly under his arm.

"You can't park there, man." He casually strides over. When he gets a clearer look of my face, his grin grows smug. "Hey, it's you, man. I knew you'd come see old Guy again."

He unlocks the door and helps me out. The tyres were damaged from the Hospital explosion. We had broken down across London Bridge, almost made it to the other side. Just my luck. I unlock the back cab doors and help Mia down.

"What's with the eye shadow, man?" he asks me.

"Nothing," I quickly respond.

Guy spots Mia in her hospital gown. I take off my jacket and wrap her around in it for decency's sake. "Whoa is that your lady?"

"Shut up, Guy!" I screech back.

"If you, like, need a quick getaway. I got a car."

"Thanks, but we're okay." As soon as I say this, the black SUVs used by Clover come into view. "Where are your wheels…? Guy." I struggle to force the words through my grating teeth.

Guy leads us down a wide back alley, showing an obvious car-shaped object hidden underneath a tarp. He rips it off, and underneath the flapping fabric is a black 2019 Dodge Charger. A muscle car I've only seen in the movies.

"May I introduce you to Gungarok," Guy exclaims.

"Gungarok?" I say with a hint of sarcasm.

"Yeah, man. Look at the number plate." He insists on showing us and goes to great measure to draw our attention to his personalised plate.

Sure enough, it was 'GNG4R0K'. "Impressive," I grit.

"Thanks, man."

"So how can a man who sells drugs and pornography afford a muscle car like this?"

Mia shouts, "It doesn't matter. Get in."

We all enter the car. Guy drives, with Mia in the passenger seat and me in the back. The seats were smooth red leather as the primary and grey as the secondary colours. I'll give Guy credit; I didn't hate the car at all.

"So, where to?" Guy breaks the silence.

"Guildford," I say.

"What? Why?" Mia chimes in. "If we're being hunted, why would we go home where our families are?"

"Because I need to see Doctor Wells."

"Why?"

"Because she knows my secret and is responsible for us only knowing now. She poisoned me."

"You're dying?" Mia sounds worried.

"No… Yes."

Mia hits me with her hands. "How are you only telling me this now?"

"I'm thinking of how to survive, Mia, give me some goddamm slack."

A silence befalls the cabin.

"You two need serious couple's counselling?" Guy breaks the tension.

"Dante," Mia begins. "This jacket, it says property of Dan Swash inside."

I slam my head on the stained-glass window in defeat. An epiphany befalls me whilst I mope. Doctor Wells knows about Godly biology, perhaps she can cure me of Apate's poison! I just need to find the right persuasion.

After a long silence on the road, I turn to Guy, who I've only met once before, and didn't even talk to him, who is now risking his life to smuggle us out of the city.

"Why are you helping me, Guy? We barely know each other."

"Because I love adventure, man. Besides, us low life petty criminals gotta stick together, know what I'm saying?"

I don't answer. The last guy who wanted to accompany me on an adventure, was torn in half in front of me.

Luckily, none of the authorities know we're travelling in this car. We leave the city. Finally. A trip to the capital I'll never forget (but certainly want to). We followed the road along the A3. Past the M25 motorway and stop in the small town of Ripley. The radio buzzes into life. "We apologise for any inconvenience we might have just caused, but the Prime Minister has a message that will now be broadcast on all frequencies and mediums, radio, television or via internet. Thank you," the broadcaster's voice instructs.

Soon, the voice of Alex Pines, Prime Minister of The UK, begins his speech.

"Good afternoon. Today is a day that has unfortunately been written into the history books. Never has the safety, or normality, of the British people, and by extension the world, been so drastically shifted. A few days ago, the concept of super powers, was the thing of fiction and entertainment. But now, we have learnt that there are powers greater than ourselves in this world.

"The events of the past few days. From the welcoming town of Guildford, to the streets of our great capital city, have forced us all to make a change in how we live for the better and safety of our great country.

"I urge you all to report any anomalous activity to the following number that will soon be messaged to your mobile devices.

"I would also like to tell you the progress we have made in identifying this 'Man in Black' involved in the incidents. This strange character has a name now. Dante Adler." Mia and myself give each other a worrying look of disbelief. "A picture of Dante Adler will be posted soon. If you spot him. Please do not approach. We do not know if he means any harm. Just report any sighting.

"Thank you and have a pleasant rest of your day."

The frequency cuts off and is soon replaced by Wham's 'Wake me up before you go-go' playing on Radio 1. I'm too shocked at the sudden thorn that has now been stabbed into the abdomen of my life, to even breathe right now.

"Whoa." Guy looks straight at me. "Wonder who that guy is?"

Chapter 13

Suffering

My identity had been exposed. It lasted… Hold on, just let me check my imaginary watch… Yep, just what I thought, about a day and a half.

The whole country now knows that yours truly is a super powered dude, and they don't know if they should welcome me with open arms, or start a witch hunt.

The worst part now is what to do next. I was going to confront Doctor Wells (Who has been prescribing me with the omnitoxike medication since I was a boy) and find out what she knows. Now I just need a place to lie low.

Guy was very surprised when I told him that I was 'the' Dante Adler.

"Whoa. What'd you do, man?" he questions.

We were parked and still seated in Guy's car, which he calls Gungarok. Even if I don't catch anyone's attention, Mia was still in a hospital gown and wearing a biker's jacket. Something that was sure to catch wandering eyes.

"Is there a hotel or Premier Inn nearby?" I ask to anyone who would listen.

Guy strokes the few whiskers on his chin. Mia shrugs.

"I'll check my phone. The Rozzers have no idea I'm even with you. So won't be tracking my phone," Guy pitches in.

"That's a plan," Mia adds. I nod in agreement.

Monty's Place was a small little bed and breakfast family run business operating in Ripley. It served dual functions as a pub and inn. Serving classic British cuisine like Fish and Chips with a pint of Guinness, and allowing weary travellers a spot to lay their heavy heads after a long hard day trip's drive.

Guy had a suspiciously healthy amount of cash in his glove compartment, and used this to pay for a night's stay.

He also went into town to buy both myself and Mia fresh clothes from a local M&S. I just got a fresh pair of grey trousers and a thin dark navy-blue hoodie to slip on underneath my biker jacket. Mia however got a whole lot more variety. She got a red lumberjack's shirt and overalls, making her look like a typical American country girl about to pull out a bass guitar and play a song in a barn.

As 'Gungarok' (I can't believe that's what I'm calling it now) is no suitable place to change clothes, we sneak into some public toilets to use the cubicles to change.

I lock the cubicle and sit on the lid of the toilet seat. As far as I could tell, no one else was heeding nature's call in these clearly uncared-for public toilets. I'm pretty sure I can tell what the strangely coloured pigments between the floor tiles are.

It was surprisingly difficult to take off my once clean and now blood-stained hoodie. My arms were shaking, like I was about to have an anxiety attack. It was still surreal to see no cuts or bruises along my arms.

The ripped trousers were even more difficult to slip off. The wound I sustained from Apate was getting tender and sore again. I'd almost convinced myself that the purple cut wasn't even there, but it would soon get worse and worse, until finally making me bite the dust.

The new clothes fit me quite well, maybe a slice bit big but nothing truly aggravating.

I leave the cubicle and walk to the lane of sinks with a massive mirror covering the wall and wash my hands.

"Dante."

I recognise that voice, but not the tone. I look forward to the reflected image of myself in the mirror, but it wasn't all me.

It was me, sure, but covered in blood and cuts and bones sticking out of a multitude of places. My left eye was ghost pale as if it were blind.

"Virgil," I reply.

"In the flesh."

"How are you there. Your voice is no longer coming from my head? Or shouting for that matter?"

"Just a part of the connection growing stronger. Now we can look into each other's soul. Eye to eye." He laughs after that point. "Who am I kidding? I don't have a soul."

I try to wave my hand, but my reflection doesn't copy me. "Why have you been ignoring me?" I ask it.

"No reason." I don't believe that. "Just been working out what our next move should be."

My dark reflection scratches the basin in front of him. "I hope you're not losing focus."

"What does that mean?"

"Well…" Virgil raises his hand to his face, examining his newly sharpened claws. "Three is a crowd. Two I can tolerate."

"I'm not just going to abandon Guy. He's helped us this far."

"Observe the clock, Dante. Observe the clock."

I lose my patience, "Enough of your cryptic bullshit! Tell me what you want?"

"The Hallowed solstice is almost upon us, Dante."

"Whatever that means," I spite back.

"It occurs once every four hundred and forty-five years on Halloween night. When the realms of the living and dead are closest when super positioned in space-time. Allowing the easiest travel between the worlds. That's why Halloween is associated with scary shit. Demons and monsters crossing over to our domain. It is no coincidence that Brunhilda and her group want your wife before the solstice."

"Why?"

"I don't know yet." He shrugs his shoulders, then begins sharpening his claws on the reflected basin again.

I take my old, torn clothes and shove them down the bin violently, then begin to make my way out.

"I'm not done yet, Dante," he calls out. "If you're half as smart as you think you are now; you'll ditch the junkie." I don't answer. Virgil gets agitated and begins banging on his side of the mirror. "Observe the clock. Trust no one!"

A smashing sound rings through the toilet halls. I look behind to find smashed mirror pieces spread over the tiled floor as if it were a Banksy art piece. Somehow, a voice in my head can now talk to me via reflective surfaces and impact the outside world. I'm now starting to question Virgil's allegiance. To me, my friends and family. Or to himself and his unhealthy obsession with saving the world.

The atmosphere in the dining area of the pub was rowdy for the time of day. It was just past two o'clock in the afternoon, but the customers treated it like it was ten p.m.

They were getting rowdy, singing 'Sweet Caroline', despite that being primarily a football chant, and no football was being played on the TV. A group of young adults were having a drinking contest to see who could chug their pint the quickest, then place the empty glass on their heads. After their match, they toasted.

"To Dante Adler! Top geezer!" The whole pub sings and repeats the chant.

It's clear now. They're all getting pissed to celebrate me. Oh joy.

I squeeze my way through the crowd to the bar side. "Which way to the rooms?"

"That way, up the stairs. The floor with purple velvet carpet." He points down a hall, then returns to cleaning a cup with a clean rag.

Our room was number 04. It only had one single bed, so Guy brought two extra sleeping bags for me and him. We were gentlemen (at least I was) and let Mia take the semi-comfy mattress.

We also bought a game of scrabble to play whilst hiding out. The sun was starting to set. Soon my time will be up, and The Acolytes will come for us again, and yet I still haven't told Mia her part in the story.

"A-S-S. Ass." Guy places the tiles on the game board, and inadvertently sets the tone for the rest of the game.

Mia fiddles the worded pieces through her fingertips. "S-A-N-D. Sand."

It was now my turn. I look at the words I have. They form alongside one another on the floor, spelling 'Charon'. An image flashes in my head of a demon made of charred wood and fire. My instincts make me kick the pieces and game board aside.

"I'm sorry," I softly speak.

"Are you okay?" Mia tries to reassure me by holding me, but I wiggle free.

"I just need some space."

Guy grabs Mia gently, as if to protect her. "Come on, Mia. Let's get some food."

They both exit the room, leaving me with my troubled thoughts, and Virgil's cackling Hyena laugh.

It rained with rumbling thunder and scratching lightning that night. I went to sleep in the bag not too long after the others left. My body woke myself up as if it sensed something. The digital clock on the bedside table said 23.59 p.m. I swear I could hear the ticking, despite the evident fact that no such digital analogue ticks or tocks.

00.00. The ticking stops.

"Time's run out, Dante."

I know that voice. It's Guy. He's standing in the doorway, motionless. Not even looking like he is breathing.

"Where's Mia?" I cautiously ask.

"Nearby. What's your answer?"

"Excuse me?"

Guy smirks, he builds up a bile of snot and saliva in the back of his throat and spits it out on the floor. The bile was black and inky. He was an Acolyte all this time. "I think you know."

I try to make a quick U-turn and dash out of the window, but 'Guy' was quicker than I was. A slash befalls my nape. I try to put pressure on it, but my body grows weak and limp. My legs start to shake. The left side of my body tingles and feels like I'm having a stroke.

I can't stay up. I fall on my back onto the mattress. Paralysed. I can't even blink.

'Guy' sits himself on top of me, like a masseuse, and begins to rub my chest, sensually. "Such a waste of a body. If only you took the mistress's offer. Then we wouldn't be here, would we?"

My head slumps to the right. "Look at me when I'm talking to you." He grabs my head and turns it towards him. "There. That's better."

My captor then slips off the beanie that is on his head. Revealing a zipper at the base of his hairline. He begins to unzip, pulling it downward towards his brow, but it snaps off.

"Oh dear. This disguise is so cheap. Forgive my lack of professionalism. This is going to be ugly." He winks and tosses the small discarded metal aside.

He sinks his fingers into his forehead with both hands and begins to pull. His human face was being ripped in half. It made a sound similar to cloth being ripped and organs being squashed. A mixture of red human blood and the black ink droops and pours itself onto my face, getting into my eyes, making them itchy.

Eventually, the whole of 'Guy' was no more. The wasted skin was left on the floor like a dirty pair of clothes.

The entity towered over me. It resembled a woman who had been mummified three thousand years ago, and was decorated with barbed wire intertwined between her muscles and tendons. Her fingers resembled rusty scissors that could cut through brick.

"Oizys. Avatar of suffering. Pleased to meet you." It spoke with a silver and slippery tongue. The signature black ink drooling out of all sorts of orifices and openings along her prickly body.

She leans in closer to my face. Her breath stinks of fish guts and offal. The slick tongue limps out of her mouth and she licks across my entire face like a snake or eel. All I could do was make a slight groan.

"Very sweet." She licks her lips. "Like butterscotch."

Her attention then turns to my left hand; she raises it up towards her. "You know, I'm glad you decided to decline the mistress' offer. Means I have free rein to do this."

My ring finger is singled out. Her fingers were as cold as the metal they were made of. She placed my finger between two of hers, and began to squeeze.

The pain was torture. I knew she planned on taking the whole finger. I'd beg her to just do it quickly if I could. But being helpless to her ways is part of the torment.

Snip.

My finger fell and rolled off the bed. My wedding ring pinged off and rolled under some of the furniture, I think. I couldn't move to see where it stopped in its tracks.

"Oh dear." She leans over the side of the bed and picks up my severed finger. "Wasted goods. Boohoo." The mummified woman then flings the finger over the back of her shoulder without a care in the world.

Without a moment's reprieve, she grabs my arms and digs her fingers into my flesh. Blood rippling out like wet paint on a canvas.

"It feels good to grab your flesh." The blades dig deeper, touching my nerves, sending fiery agony up to my pain receptors. "You know, in our past lives, we were lovers once. Our passion, etched into the sands of ancient Egypt. Our love built the great pyramids. But you don't remember that do you? You used me. Turned me into this… thing!" She lets go and slashes me across the face, leaving five definable lines of each finger from left to right.

She then lowers her face to mere millimetres from my own. Her stagnant breath even more putrid at this proximity "Are you even in there? Bek?"

She hovers over as if waiting for a response.

The door swings open with a kick, averting Oizys' gaze.

Standing in the doorframe, illuminated by lights in the hall, was Mia, wielding a pump action shotgun like Sarah Connor in Terminator Two.

"Get the hell away from him, you bitch!"

Oizys hisses, but Mia is playing no games. She fires bullet after bullet into the wailing creature. I can see the green flashes of the pellets springing from the barrel of the gun to the ancient corpse of suffering.

Wait. Green?

Oizys crashes through the window after taking much damage and disappears into the dark rain like a phantom memory.

Mia rushes to my side. "Dante? Dante?" She shakes me profusely. The thing with being fully paralysed is you can't express how grateful you are to the people who save you.

Two more silhouettes enter the room, as they get closer, I can tell they resemble Men in Black with their business suits and sunglasses.

Clover.

"These men helped me. They said they can help you as well," Mia explains.

I grunt in disagreement. More people come in. Ambulance workers with a stretcher and neck brace. They strap me in, harshly, violently and tightly, I think I detect a hint of prejudice, and roll me out.

The pub was evacuated as far as I could tell. No singing or chanting that I could hear. Outside, the rain dropped on my head. Thunder and lightning brightened the sky above me. The sounds of the agents' leather boots against the ground alongside me sounded like an army march.

I think I'm beginning to get a bit of sensation back in my right arm. I try to move it, but an agent clasps it down.

“Please. We don’t want you to do any more damage.” The agent gives a wide fake smile.

I try to squint my eyes to see where Mia is, she is right behind me, wearing a coat that Clover must have given her.

I wish I could scream or shout, *they are not our friends! They’ll lock us up and do experiments on us!* But only I can hear my own stupid rattling voice.

They load me up into an ambulance, but it looks more like a prisoner transfer vehicle. No medical equipment or friendly healthcare workers. Just grey walls, a couple of tubes and syringes of I don’t even know what, and two men in riot armour, holding batons.

Mia was directed into another vehicle.

One of the guards leans over to speak to me. “Don’t try anything stupid.” He finishes his statement with hitting me in the eye with the butt on his baton.

I moan with discomfort and make a promise in my head.

I’ll kill him first.

Chapter 14

Powerless

The whole journey was uncomfortable. The guards just talked about girls with huge asses or the hottest celebrities. Sleazy douchebags.

At any point I try to move, wiggle, or even blink, I get a taste of the baton. After a brief breath of silence after my last hit, more topics are brought up for conversation between my two guardsmen.

"Got any slayer stories?" One guard asks the other.

Slayer stories?

"My dad met Reginald Graves once."

"Oh shit, the treasure hunter?"

"Yeah, his team were hunting for the remains of El Dorado in the eighties. They believed that Midas, the guy that turned anything he touched to gold, might be buried there. Sure enough, they found the city in the Amazon and the coffin of Midas."

"Doesn't Midas' file say he frequently went to parties with the Olympians?"

"No, that wasn't him. Can't remember who," The storytelling guard continues, "So they were going to take one of his hands right, for safekeeping and study. But Graves swoops in, blows up the coffin and the remains and, guess what?"

"What?" the listening guard says excitedly.

"Graves sinks the entire city back into the swamps."

"Why?"

"I think my dad said that he said it was cursed gold and a trap for humanity or something like that. But I bet Graves took some gold for himself."

"Fucking slayers, man."

"That's right." The guard looks straight at me with fiery eyes. "Fucking slayers."

What I wouldn't give to hear Mia's stories about old school friends shoving vegetables up places they should never go in the first place.

At least it sounds like I was a badass in my past life, like a cross between James Bond and Indiana Jones.

The transport stopped with a jolt. Even the guards rocked side to side abruptly. They opened the back doors and wheeled me out on the stretcher.

The sun was a crimson orange. The sky, a pale yellow, as if an angry snow storm were on the way. It still rained gently and silently. A ringing thunder could be heard grumbling over the horizon.

I couldn't tell what building they were taking me to. I still couldn't move my neck thanks to the brace.

"Where is she?" I ask.

My escorts don't answer and continue to manoeuvre me inside.

The ceiling was blue. That much I can tell. It sounded lively as well, people rushing from one place to the other, like it was never a dull or leisurely day, wherever we were.

After a brief elevator trip down to the extra low floor underground, I'm wheeled off into a new padded cell room like an Asylum's. My captors unfasten the straps and restraints, remove my neck brace, stick some sort of syringe in my nape, then kick me off the stretcher. Still one of my more comfortable landings in recent memory.

The cell door is sealed behind me with a massive clang. Whatever was in that syringe, I summarised, was to keep me mortal for a while longer. Barring me from my abilities. It also made me dizzy, like vertigo dialled up to eleven.

My vision was vibrant, yet unfocused. One moment, the walls look like they're closing in, the next, like they're twisting away like a spring.

My ankle wound felt like it was getting worse. The temporary measures taken at the Vet practice were beginning to wear off. Meaning soon I'd be dead as a Dodo.

After a noticeable expanse of time (at least from my intoxicated perspective), the cell door locks click open. A group of armoured guards, similar to the ones in the transport, drag me out of the cell, hauling me up by my arms with my feet scraping across the hard floor as they take me.

"Where is she?" I gobble again. No reply.

I'm chucked into a new room; it looks similar to an interrogation room. Same two-way mirror. Same metal table and chairs. Same asshole about to probe into my head sitting in one said chair.

"Howdy, Dante," said the smug Tom Grayson.

I begin to pick myself up, sleazily and unfocused like. I trip into my empty chair. Tom watches with enthusiasm as I rest myself on the steel chair.

"Wasn't too long ago we were in a similar position," he begins.

"Where is she?" I groan.

"We offered you help, and you spat in our face."

"Where… is… she?"

"Now the whole world is going to shit. With you as its poster boy."

"Please…"

"Death's Acolytes, a warrior angel, and the abandoned bastard son of Zeus. We could have helped, and reduced the damage you and this cast of characters caused in your little game of cat and mouse."

I hit the table with as much power as my fist can muster forth. "Where is she!"

Tom raises his index finger and places it on his mouth, shushing me. He then points to an overhead clock above us. 09.32 a.m. "Observe the clock, Dante."

That quote is the exact same as Virgil stated earlier.

"Today is the Hallowed Solstice. I'm sure your little 'Jiminy Cricket' has told you what that means?"

I nod in acknowledgement. "Yes."

"The realm of the dead is just footsteps away. Interdimensional travel of sorts on a much smaller scale. Monsters scurrying their way to our world to quench their monstrous fetishes and appetites. It's not right."

"Are you trying to persuade me to join your super-secret boy band again?"

"No. That ship has sailed and well and truly sunk." Tom pulls up a file on his tablet and slides it over to me. "Look here now."

I pick up the device and squint to look at the writing and images. I can piece together what the picture is, a bomb.

"A bomb."

"Yes, Dante, and you and your wife are the final piece of the equation."

"You threatening me, agent?"

"Yes. You see, Dante, the realm is a dark reflection of our own, a near perfect mirror image. You could pop in at one location and easily come back to our world and end up in a different continent if you know how to traverse the terrain. That access is a danger to worldwide security. Foreign or domestic. Monsters or man.

For too long, monsters have traversed here, terrorised humanity. Vampires, Werewolves or some other kind of cursed force have tried to make Earth their summer home.

Tonight. This bomb will end the realm in a hurray of fireworks like the fourth of July."

Grayson sounds like a madman. Blowing up an entire realm? What would the repercussions be?

"You can't blow up an entire dimension."

"We can and we will. For the safety of humanity."

"But this is the realm of the dead! Ending that will do… I don't even know what!"

"We have plans on how to procced accordingly after the detonation."

"What about the souls of the dead?"

"Doesn't matter. They're dead after all."

I pull off a brave face. "I won't let you rape the natural order of things."

Tom pulls a face back. "You won't even live to see it through."

After a pause, I answer back. "Where is my wife?"

"Don't worry, you and your wife will be reunited soon." Tom grabs his tablet back and pulls up a new file, he shows it to me. It looks like scribbles in a language I don't recognise, from a book too old to exist. It does however show a drawing, like primitive stick figures. Two people, standing opposite one another, holding hands. In the foreground behind them, it looks like a swirling portal with harshly scribbled clawed hands reaching out of it.

"What is this?"

"That, Dante, is the ritual for opening the land of the dead during the solstice. Two lovers, sacrificed in blood, under the residence of a holy place. The very deed of this, tears a rip in space-time. Opening the door, to the other side."

"This is…" I lose the capacity to speak after that. I was trying to say evil, but the words were too frightened to leave my lips.

"You and your wife, will die today."

"Why are you telling me this?"

Tom stands and radios for the guards, using the walkie talkie on his hip. "When we first met. I meant that I was trying to help you. Now you've crossed my organisation, using you and your whore wife, who also happens to be part God, as part of the ritual, is beneficial. It's killing two birds with one stone. My partner died yesterday, fighting you. I want you to suffer, knowing you can't do anything to stop us."

I stand too. I'm not afraid. "I may not be able to stop you right now, but there are things coming for me that can."

"What do you mean?" Tom asks nervously.

I laugh. "Brunhilda gave me till today to cooperate with her gang. A deal. They want Mia. They'll come for us. In anger. Did I not mention that?"

As soon as I finish, the alarm system goes off. Perfect timing. The guards burst in. I begin to laugh manically, and I love it.

"Get him back to his cell, cuff him."

The two guards sling a tight pair of cuffs on my wrists, and begin to shove me out into the hall and back towards my cell.

The atmosphere begins to rumble. Dust shakes off the ceiling like we were in the midst of an earthquake.

"Scared, lads?" I ask the guards. They don't answer, or even strike me in retaliation for asking me questions. They're scared. Good.

My cell was coming up on the right. The leading guard took out a key from his back pocket. I begin to struggle against my escort, head-butting the guard with the key. Cracking his visor and felling him. All my bottled rage gave me strength. I flip over the guard behind me, wrapping the chains of my cuffs around his neck, and begin to strangle him. He chokes on his own tongue and he falls too.

I grab the keys to my cuffs off of the guard and unbind myself. At this point, you'd think I should use my voltaic whips, but when I try to ignite them, it gives me a harsh electric shock and burn. Mortal muscles must not be able to withstand the current. It would be best to not get into any form of conflict until I can reconnect to my power.

I knew I was underground, but underground what? That was the question.

I make my way to the elevator, there is no one in the way, they must be busy with whatever is going on upstairs.

Luckily no one was in the elevator. I push the button titled 'LG', assuming that means 'lower ground' floor. The elevator played a little melodic jingle as it rose. I didn't notice that the first time I came in through here.

The doors slide open. Before me lies carnage and debris. Agents' heads exploded, their bodies lying on the floor. Splatter marks were spread across the walls, probably from their once whole heads, until they went pop. The hallways were filled with dust that rose like smoke in a fire. The lights were flickering blue. I could hear the sound of gunshots, and quickly hid in a room whose door was open.

Inside the room, were fifteen screen monitors plastered across the wall, showing different places and angles throughout this complex. This was the security room.

Looking at the monitors, I could see what looked like thick black webs and human shaped cocoons on the second floor.

On the third floor, there was a shape that was moving too quickly to perceive.

The footage on the ground floor was most disturbing. Agents firing their guns which should hurt Godly influenced beings. A figure was approaching. It looked like a ghost made of smoke. The bullets passed straight through it. As it walked closer to the agents, their heads would explode. At least that answers the question on what killed those people outside.

The ghost stopped in its bloody path, it looked straight into the camera, as if it knew it were being watched. It quickly evaporated. I think it's coming here.

I quickly make my exit back into the hallway, amongst the dead bodies. That's it! I hide myself under a pile of bodies. Disgusting, but it's my best shot at evasion.

The ghost reappears in front of me. It doesn't know I'm hiding amongst the cadavers. It looks inside the security room. Angered at losing its prey, it destroys the monitors in a flurry of sparks and tosses the swivel chair that the staff would have used around like a balloon.

The smoke emanating smells like tar, its stench is more potent than the bodies. The being exits and smoulders into a cloud of smoke and whisks off.

It was clear now, as I stood up, these things were the remaining Acolytes I had not had the displeasure of meeting yet. My one concern now was finding Mia and leaving this place.

I search every room on this floor. Every nook and cranny, for Mia, but all I find are coffee break rooms or empty cells. The odd interrogation room, here and there.

I was now on the ground floor, crouched and silently pacing along.

"Mia?" I'd call out at odd intervals, to no reply.

I recognised this giant lobby I was in now; the ceiling was easy to identify when it was all you could look at for a while. By the looks of this place, it's actually a police station, but which? I don't know.

But there was more to this lobby then meets the eye, silky black webs hung from the ceiling like thick vines in the Amazon Jungle. More of the cocoons were scattered across the floor and walls. Curiosity got the better of me. I kneel down to one of the cocoons and rip it open with my hands. Inside was someone who looked like all the water from his body had been drained from his body, like a human raisin.

It's strange. I feel indifferent. No sympathy. No emotion at all to the plight of this poor person. I just get up and carry on with my mission.

Another thing to note, was that the entrance had been barred shut by some sort of reinforced metal shielding. It probably kicked in when the station was under attack. Clover must use this place regularly if they have protective measures like this and super-secret underground floors.

I make my way up a flight of stairs to the first floor. It looked like a large room with rows of office cubicles, each with its own unique personalised desk.

"Mia?" I try again.

"Dante?" I hear a response.

Mia pokes her head from underneath a desk, and on realising it's me, scurries out from under and embraces me.

"I'm so sorry," she profusely exaggerates.

"It's okay, you didn't know what these guys were. It's okay." I hold her tight. "Listen to me. They're here for you."

"What?"

"I promise I will tell you everything, but now we have to get out!"

A sudden clicking noise echoes from behind us.

Click! Click! Click!

I shove Mia underneath the desk and quickly follow underneath. The clicking grows louder.

A pair of heavy and furry feet walk past us. Four long bristly appendages were being dragged behind it like snakes. I ease forward on my stomach to get a better look.

It was a giant man-spider hybrid. Big and covered in bristles. The four appendages were spider legs. Its face was disgusting! It had huge mandibles with razor fangs. It had four eyes on its face. All human, but sad. The arms had retractable blades made of bone sticking out of its forearm.

The hybrid jumped onto the ceiling and began to crawl. I take this opportunity to begin to sneak, taking Mia's hand in my own. The spider kept crawling, it twisted its head a hundred and eighty degrees to keep an eye on the ground whilst it crawled.

We hide against the panels of one of the cubicles to hide from the spider's eye line. I grab what looks like a bobble head of John Travolta from Grease from a desk and throw it in the opposite direction.

The spider clicks its mandibles again and pounces in the direction of the distraction.

We quickly scurry, but the monster pounces in front of us, crossing us off from our point of exit. It still doesn't see us, so we quickly crawl to the left through an open glass door leading to the conference room. It had a large oval table with many cheap brown plastic chairs tucked underneath.

Hiding underneath the great table felt annoying to me. I want to just fight. How much longer do I have to wait till I'm powered up again?

The spider pounces on top of the oval table. Mia gasps, but quickly covers her mouth.

Click! Click! Click!

Its claws scratched on the oak of the table. I can't tell if it knows we're here and is just toying with us.

Suddenly, I feel a wave of power flood me internally. I must have my powers back. I punch the air and turn my wrist, fully igniting the whip in a blaze and sending both the table and spider monster flying upward into the ceiling.

"Run!" I shout at Mia.

We quickly get to our feet and sprint out back into the office room. I suddenly trip. Looking at my feet, I see them wrapped in the black webs, with the strand leading to the spider's mouth, who had now recovered from my hit.

"Dante!" Mia screams back.

"Just go!"

Mia keeps running and escapes. The spider grasps his strand with his prickly hands and begins to yank me towards him. I try to ignite another whip, but the spider shoots another web out of its mouth and binds both my hands together, rendering any attack of mine useless now.

The spider brings me closer. "Know your death came at the hands of Moros."

But before my death could come, a spray of fire extinguishing foam surprises Moros the spider, and renders him vulnerable briefly from the cold. He drops me and quickly retreats himself.

Mia drops the empty extinguisher and starts ripping the webs from my body.

"You came back?"

"Well you know. Marriage vows and all that." She hides her fear with humour.

"I told you to run."

"You don't tell me what to do."

"Your stubbornness could have gotten you killed."

Mia rips the last of the webs from my feet, allowing me to stand. She tries to help with the black silky substance around my hands, but I pull away and use the heat from my birthing whips to boil the webs, frying them and blasting them off in a flurry of art.

"Come on." I reach to grab Mia's hand but she pulls away.

"I don't need you to hold my hand." She paces first and leaves the room. I follow.

The lobby was still as empty as a graveyard. The security shield doors were still active. I wrap my arm with a blood whip, using it as makeshift padding, ready to bust a hole through the shield.

Bam!

A dent? That's all? I try again. Same result. "Fuck," I outburst.

"What now?" Mia asks.

I don't know, but I don't tell her that. I try hitting the

reinforced metal again. Dent. The shielding must be forged with some sort of anti-god magic or trickery.

"Perhaps there's a switch to lower the defences," I finally come up with.

"What about the power?"

"I'm sure the generators are more than capable of running defences, even when damaged."

Just then, even the flickering lights were snuffed out. It was pitch black. The power had been severed.

"Dante," Mia cries out.

"I'm here." I reach for one of my centipede bracelets, perform the little wrist movement ritual to kickstart one, and a small stream sparks out, I grab it and gently pull on it lightly like string and wrap it around my hand.

It felt warm on my hand, like reassurance. It began to softly light up the room. It was my own personal torch.

Mia briefly shielded her eyes. "What do we do?"

After much thought and contemplation "I don't know." I finally reply.

If there is no power whatsoever, that means no electricity is coming from the grid, and places like this would have back-up generators, and since no lights came on, that means they have more than likely been destroyed by the creatures.

Then, I realize that there might be someone who does know what to do.

"We have to find Tom Grayson."

Chapter 15

Uneasy

"Are you fucking serious? Why would he help us?" Mia questions.

"Because, like most animals, he will show the habit of 'self-preservation', meaning he will do whatever it takes to survive. And I will persuade him to help."

"How do we know he's even still alive?"

I tap into my power to listen to Clover radio frequencies, by closing my eyes and concentrating. Focusing on the individual walkie talkie, that absorbs Grayson's voice when he speaks into it and distributes it out to the others.

Bzzzz. "Is anyone there?" *Bzzzz.* "This is Agent Grayson; I am on the third floor. Need immediate assistance. Does anyone copy?"

I open my eyes. "Found him. He's alive. Third floor"

"How do you… You know what, doesn't matter. Let's go."

We take the walk towards the nearest flight of stairs very slowly and cautiously, like we were in a booby-trapped tomb from Indiana Jones. The slightest misstep, and the whole thing goes boom!

My whip light was actually quite efficient. It glowed better and brighter than some handhelds at home, but whatever is lurking in the shadows can see us too, like a giant bullseye, but we had to take that chance.

We reached the spiralling staircase, it looked wet and slippery, like there had been a leak in the roof and no one had bothered to call it in.

I took the first step, and indeed it was as uneasy as stepping on ice. I had to hold the banister to steady myself. I reached out my hand and offered to help keep Mia stable as she walked up, she accepted my help.

We repeated this cycle all the way to the third floor.

"So which way now?" Mia asks me.

I close my eyes and listen for a frequency. The buzzing sounds loudest down towards the evidence lockers. "This way." And off we went.

The evidence lockers were sealed behind a massive vault door like it was a high-profile bank on Wall Street. Who knows what contraband they've acquired that requires a bank vault lock. It had a fingerprint scanner next to it.

Without hesitation, I look at the ground for any bodies. A well-preserved hand was sticking out of a pile of cadavers like a golden goose.

As I pulled, a few tendons and nerves were still attached to the rest of the body and one by one pinged and snapped. Mia looked like she was holding back the urge to be sick.

I place the palm on the scanner. Nothing.

"They need electricity to work," Mia comments.

A fit of rage befalls me. I rip the scanner off, exposing the wires and plunge my lighted fist into the circuitry.

"Welcome, Agent," a synthesised voice beckons. The vault door hinges open.

"Guess my body electricity gave enough juice to override it," I joke.

Inside, the room felt bigger than the rest of the entire building. We could see rows and rows of items of unimaginable description stacked up like trophies.

I think I pieced together a watch with unrecognisable planets instead of numbers.

A live Eagle in a terrarium, wearing a business suit and glasses.

A collection of foetuses in jars of preserving alcohol. They looked like a variety of hybrid monsters.

The skeleton of a giant winged creature, and many more.

"Grayson!" I call out into the dark.

I hear movement to my right, move my light to get a clearer view. I see Tom Grayson shaking in his boots.

"Dante?" He quickly repositions himself to look firmer and more collected. "How did you find me?"

"Followed the sound of shaking bones," I sarcastically say.

Mia walks into our conversation.

"I see you found your wife." Tom pretends to sound pleased.

"Shut up, asshole!" Mia responds.

Tom straightens his tie, unsure of what to do. "I see why the two of you are a couple."

I walk closer to Tom, and shine the light in his face. "How do we get out?"

"Through the front door."

I say nothing, but stare. Tom straightens his tie again. "There's no electricity running through the building. These Acolytes are smart."

"Wait, Dante used his whip things to briefly hotwire the vault door. Can't we do something similar to the generators?" Mia asks.

"No. The electricity coursing through the whips, is not

powerful enough to jumpstart our generators. They're 'special', besides the vault's security is primitive in comparison. Doesn't require nearly enough volts," Tom explains.

"I know both you and your little organisation well enough that you have another exit," I explain.

Tom gulps. "There is another way."

"Then take us to it," Mia demands.

"Now why would I do that?"

"A truce. I will protect you. You lead us to this way out. After that. It's back to the old ways." I give him my terms.

"You should know, it's not a typical way out."

"Tell us," Mia chimes again.

"Will you shut up and let me finish!" Mia nods. "It's a sort of train. It'll take us to our head lab. It has an external power supply that only a few know about, so it won't be affected by the power cut. It's where we made the toxin to supress your powers."

"Okay, where is this secret entrance?" I ask.

"In the break room, behind the vending machine. It's an old door that's been covered with wallpaper, so we don't need to worry about sci-fi technological locks."

I shove him in front of us. "You lead."

Tom rolls his eyes. "But I can't see shit."

I rest my palm on the nape of his neck, and gently wrap my fingers around his neck. I lower my glow hand nearer his eyes. "Better?"

"…Yes."

"Just remember who's in charge."

Tom leads us down many halls, all similarly covered in carnage. "This way," he'd say from time to time. I regularly checked back to reassure myself that Mia was with us.

It was eerily quiet considering there were three murderous creatures in the building.

We finally entered what looked like a break room. There were two vending machines. One for confectionary, and one for drinks. There were three small circular tables in the centre of the room. One man had ten chocolate bars shoved down his throat, killing him. His eyes still watery.

Tom tried to move the candy machine, but struggled. "A little help?" he said to me.

I smirked. "No… No you're doing just fine."

I think I heard him curse under his breath. After much (albeit funny) struggling, Tom finally moved the machine out of the way. Sure enough, there was a slight outline of a door frame.

"Happy now?" Tom berates.

"Open it," I order.

Tom scowls and begrudgingly begins to tear at the paper. A large wooden door is revealed.

"Now, I have the key for this thing, all agents do."

But I have no time for 'key finding', I just kick it open.

"Let's go." I grab Tom and shove him inside first. It begins with a downward staircase. Old gas-powered lights hung from the ceiling and flickered to life as if motion sensitive as we walked past them. I snuffed my own whip light.

The stairs were metallic. Clanging as we trod on them. The stairs seemed to go on for miles.

Finally, they ended at another door. Tom stood to the side, and let me kick it open.

Ahead of us, stood what looked like an old green steam-powered engine train. It had one carriage and no drivers or conductors.

"Who drives it?" I ask.

"It's on autopilot. I use this key in a slot on the console and the train departs." Tom flourishes a key between his fingers. "It'll teleport us with dwarf magic, but the train needs to constantly be in motion for it to work, if it stops or breaks down during transit, we're fucked."

Suddenly, something makes me feel uneasy, like someone taking little steps on the back of my head. I try to listen. It sounds like scurrying. It's getting closer.

"Move!" I shout to the group.

But it's too late, as we run, a shadow leaps over us, blocking our escape. It looks like a giant reptilian man, with black scales and a golden stripe pattern along its back. Its snout elongated like a crocodile or Alligator.

"Looky, looky here," it snarls. "My brothers, Moros and Momus, will be so sad to know the prey is mine."

I ignite both whips with a roaring hum. I slash and slash, but the reptile is too quick. It keeps jumping and evading.

"Too slow!" it mocks me.

I formulate a plan. I turn to Tom. "Scream for me." I rip the key from his hands.

"What?" he exasperates.

I pick him up and throw him to the shadowy cold-blooded foe. The creature bites into his neck. Tom's scream echoes.

"Oh my God!" Mia screams. I pick her up and fling her over my shoulder. "You monster!" she says to me.

But I don't care. I love hearing that weasel scream in pain and anguish.

On the carriage I flip Mia onto one of the seats and slot the key into the console in the side of one of the seats.

The train sings to life with hot steam and quickly begins to turn its wheels to depart. Purple lights flicker and completely envelop the locomotive.

I look outside the window, to find not the makeshift train station, but what looks like space. Purple stars and nebulas as far as the eye can muster. I'm no scientist, but I think this is some sort of interdimensional travel, like the hallowed solstice thing. The tracks below look like blue lights. At least the croco-man can't follow us here.

The interior of the train was very oriental in design. Old fashioned, but very high class in quality. The seats were richly cushioned and green in colour. A bar with snacks and drinks were on display, next to a shelf of literature.

"Look at the stars, Mia. Beautiful." I look to Mia, but she is visibly tearing up.

"You… left him… to die."

"To save us," I reason.

"You just tossed him like bait."

"He was going to kill us!" I shout in frustration. "They were going to use us as sacrificial lambs to open some portal, blow up the realm of the dead. Every soul. Dead again. Oh, and by the way, you're related to Pandora, that crazy bitch with the box. That's why they want to kill you. And you're adopted. Your family is all fake." That felt really good to get off my chest.

Mia just shakes, then stops, she wipes the tears from her eyes and leaves to go to the seat furthest from me. "You are a monster." Were her final words.

At least this carriage has a drinks bar. I lean over and grab the biggest bottle of American Whiskey and begin to chug like a frat boy in an initiation party.

I almost forgot, I'll be dead soon if this Doctor Wells won't help me. Yeah. Almost forgot. I take another swig. The headaches are swinging back.

Chapter 16

Truth

The train ride was most uncomfortable. After my bottle of whiskey, I had a look at the books that were kept on the shelf next to the bar. It was a series of collected information about the different pantheons, like Greek, Norse, Egyptian, Hindu and more.

I take a look at the Greek book, and search for any information about the Acolytes I just encountered.

The spider was named Moros, meaning doom.

The lizard mentioned that the ghost was named Momus, meaning blame.

That means the lizard must be Nemesis, translating to retribution.

They all look different to how they are described in the stories. This must be evidence about the whole 'family' terminology. Charon chooses a new host for each avatar, if he deems them worthy. Perhaps the spider and lizard, were in fact once regular animals, but they wanted to postpone death and Charon chose them for hosts. Creepy.

The purple lights began to flicker outside, and I could feel the train beginning to slow down.

The train screeched to a halt. Outside, it looked like we were in heaven. The station was completely white and clean.

Disembarking, felt ominous. The footsteps echoed. Mia

followed after me, nudging me on her way past.

Ahead was a door, white and pure as porcelain cap teeth. It had a fingerprint scanner, but I just kicked it down, but instead of leading to a staircase, it led to a pristine hallway with glass walls. Through the glass, we could see machines with people strapped into them, like they were stuck in some sort of virtual reality headset gear.

There was also a row of people in what looked like bathtubs filled with salt and with their brains exposed with wires leading to a complex machine and showing dreams.

"What is this?" I say aloud.

A woman walks around the corner, wearing a lab coat and red spectacles. I recognise her as Doctor Grey Wells.

"No one's used the Nidavellir train in decades," she begins, but as soon as she sees the two us, she stops talking, turns and runs in the other direction.

I lasso her ankles with my whip like a cowboy and ring her in towards us. "Hi, Doctor."

"Dante, please let me explain," she begs me.

But I refuse to listen. I grab her by the neck and raise her aloft and choke her. Mia tries to pull me back and restrain my urge to maim.

"Dante, let her go!"

After looking Mia in the eyes, I comply and let the witch go. Wells gasps for breath.

"Thank you," Wells pleads.

"You better start talking. He won't listen a second time."

Wells stands. I retract my whip back into my wrist. "I never wanted you to die."

"Funny way of showing that, Doc. Poisoning me all these years."

"Just, come with me, I'll show you to my personal lab."

Wells' lab was huge. It had a pull-out bed, for when she needed to sleep, that could easily be slotted away. It had x-ray and MRI brain scans on the walls. Detailed books on biology and chemistry and a desk with a skull on it.

"Get out much?" I start with a joke.

Wells sits at her desk. "What do you want to know?"

"Why?" I demand.

The Doctor breathes in and out deeply. "I meant what I said. I never wanted to kill you. Just your myth."

"I'll say it again. Why?"

"You have caused so much pain, and death, in your crusade against the Gods. Innocents used as bait, sacrifices or tools for a means to an end. You killed my son."

"Bullshit," I snap back.

"In another life," she spites.

"…So… who are you?"

Wells holds her desk skull close like a shield. "I am Sekhmet. Egyptian Goddess of healing."

That explains her medical talent, I think to myself. "So why didn't you take your revenge against me?" I ask her.

"Because you, as an individual, are innocent of crimes committed in a past life. So I took a different approach. I tried to end the cycle of death, the Godslayer brings."

"You teamed up with Clover?"

"It was I who approached them. I left the White City after my family failed to help me after my son died, all those centuries ago. But it is not easy to avoid the eyes of Horus. I hid on Earth, wanting to start a new life as a Doctor. I constantly had to flee from one place to the other. Then I found you."

Like an entertained child listening to a story, I kneel down beside her. "And then what?"

"Even as a child. I recognised your red hair and wicked aura. I contacted Clover, when I was sure. In exchange for information about you and a promise, they would protect me from the Gods."

"What did you promise?"

"That I would kill you." She wipes away a tear. "That's what all these people are used for here. Dream Therapy on the homeless and disenfranchised to become atheists. People who society would not notice or care if they disappeared. We take their dreams and refine them into anti-god uses, like weaponry or pharmaceuticals That's what omnitoxike is made of."

"But you didn't kill me."

"No. I lied to them. Told them I could not synthesise an agent that could kill you."

"But you could?"

"Yes. I could. But I took a vow to never take a life."

I finally stand. "Thank you."

Grey Wells smiles, thankful that I show appreciation for her struggle. "I take omnitoxike too, helps suppress the Godly DNA," she shares.

"Wait," I ask. "What about this bomb that Clover wants?"

Grey takes out a beats pill speaker from her desk draw. "It's this." She hands it over to Mia.

"You keep a bomb meant to blow up a dimension in your desk drawer?"

"This drawer is a pocket universe. It's bigger on the inside. It's where I keep my inventions and secrets."

"Why did you build it?"

"I have to do what they ask, or they'll expose me to my family."

"It looks different to what they showed me."

"Designs change. Take it. You deserve it more than them. You'll know what to do. Keep it out of the wrong hands."

I build up the courage to ask her for my favour. "Doctor Wells. I've been poisoned. By Apate. Could you help?" I lift up my trouser leg and show the purple slash on my ankle.

Wells looks closer and adjusts her glasses. "No."

I almost don't believe it for a second. "No?" I shout.

"The equipment required is already being used. I can't… I won't." Her eyes dart to the floor on the left, as if something is being hidden in that direction of the room.

I pace over and slam my foot on the tiled floor. It's hollow.

I smash it open, there is some sort of metal container hidden under the floor. I pull it out.

It was a small boy suspended in a pale blue liquid. He had a breathing apparatus imbedded in his face. Bubbles flowing out as he breathed.

"Your son. I presume?" I threaten.

"Please." She grovels to her knees, and begins to beg. "He's almost perfect."

"This tank will help me?"

"…Yes."

"Good."

Purr. I ready my whips, to break the thick glass.

"Wait!" Wells screams. I hesitate and turn to face her eyes. "I can try free hand."

I sheath my whips. "If it starts to go wrong. I will take that tank. Maybe, just for insurance…" I unleash a whip and wrap it around the tank, and begin to squeeze. A small crack begins to show.

"Okay. Okay. Just let me get ready."

The good Doctor rushes out to get medical equipment, leaving Mia and myself alone.

"You are not the man I married," she finally says.

I say nothing. Do I feel… Guilt?

A little while later, the operating room is prepped, and when I say operating room, I actually mean a reclining chair that I sit on, whilst my chest is cut open with sterile blades.

At least the chair is quite comfy. The Doctor hovers over me, ready to cut.

"Remember. I can squeeze at any time," I remind her and signal to the healing tank.

"…What I'm going to do is cut open your chest and ribcage, and then inject some of the healing blue liquid into your heart. It may kill you."

"Then put me in the tank."

Wells doesn't respond, and grabs a huge saw blade that looks like two people need to use it. I unzip my jackets. Ready for the cut.

The razor tips come closer to my exposed skin. I see Mia watching from outside.

Wells puts her whole body weight on the saw, and begins to carve into my chest. I scream with all the passion of an enlightened artist.

Back and forth the saw goes. Blood squirting, but I'm used to that now. My body wants to shut its eyes and die, but I won't let that happen.

Finally, the cutting is done. Wells pulls my flesh back with clamps, and reaches in to grab my heart.

She pulls out my heart, veins and arteries still connected like thick tubes. I can see the thought cross her mind of squashing my heart, but she knows I'll kill her cloned son if she even attempts it.

Wells grabs the syringe with the fluid and injects it into my heart. It feels like a rush of caffeine on steroids. I feel wide awake, flowing with new perception. My heart beats like a jackhammer.

My brain is telling me to give up and wither away, but I shout no.

The adrenaline is over. Wells places my heart back in my body, releases the clamps, and my body begins to stitch itself back together.

I release my insurance.

"Thanks." I force the words out.

"You're a monster," she replies.

Everyone says that to me now. 'You're a monster', but I'm the good guy. Right? I stop the bad guys.

"Am I cured?"

"Yes. Leave," the Doctor demands.

I do.

Mia looks somewhat happy I survived. "Are we done here?" she asks me firmly.

"Yeah."

"What now?"

"Survive. I guess"

We follow the exit signs, leading us to a pair of sliding doors, we walk through them. The air turns cold and bitter.

We recognised where we were. Guildford. Home. It was night. Halloween. It seems we just walked through Guildford Royal Surrey Hospital. I wouldn't have figured this was where Clover's secret laboratory was.

It was eerily quiet for a hospital, like every NHS staff member took holiday. Patients too.

Ahead of us we could see the gleaming lights of the Cathedral, and the scaffolding that encompassed it. I remember the website saying there was a wedding there tonight. I was planning on taking a visit there for lunch at the café. How priorities change.

The moon overhead was full and bright yellow, a bat flew above us, projecting its shadow from the light of the moon over us like a blanket. The bat stayed hovering above us. It flew closer and closer. Something was wrong. It grew larger and had arms and legs with talons and claws. Its wings were feathery, like a raven. It screeched and pounced on top of us.

"Such a shame no deal could be found." I recognised the voice. Evie Star. Brunhilda, the Valkyrie.

Its leathery arm clutched Mia and held her under its arm. It then stood over me and pressed its heel into my chest as I gobbled on the floor.

"Let her go!"

"If you want her. Fight for her." But I couldn't move or budge the serrated heel. I was trapped like a fish caught by a bird. "Such a shame." She turns her attention to Mia. "Come along dear, the covenant has big plans for you!"

She flaps her wings and sets off into the night, heading towards the Cathedral.

I can hear Mia calling my name. "Dante!"

I try to stand, but collapse from all the stress my body has recently endured.

Chapter 17

Who You Are

I drift in and out of consciousness. All I can visualise are blades of damp grass rubbing against my cheek.

I hear the sound of shovelling dirt. A spade being flipped over a stranger's head. I can't see who it is. The stranger ceases the digging and plants the spade in the earth. My blurred vision is a bane to my weary head.

The strange person grabs my ankle and rolls me into the hole. I can't move. A slave to their wishes. "Who are you?" I whimper.

The figure turns to me and draws closer. Is this the Gravedigger from my vision with Herakles? It sure looks like him. The cloak. The ominous hobby. A grey beard. My vision focuses. The image shifts. It's Wells.

"Like I said, I'll kill your myth." She begins to bury me alive with the dirt. The weight of the mud crushing down on me. Cutting off air from my lungs. Everything going black and soggy. So cold. So cold.

I feel like I'm floating. There is nothing else. Only me. Death will claim me soon, like an old friend I've avoided for too long.

"Dante," a voice cries out from the infinite nothingness.

"Who?"

"It's me." A ray of light beams like hope amongst despair. A hand grabs me and pulls me into its radiant warmth. The voice reveals itself.

"Virgil," I remark.

"Yes, Dante. It's me." Virgil assumes physical form. My pale reflection. The fresh wounds from before look like they've healed now with stitches.

We both hover in the light. "Where are we?" I ask him.

"This is your mind."

"But… why is it so dark."

"You are at a crossroads, young slayer."

"What do you mean?"

Virgil snaps his fingers, sparking an image of Brunhilda and the Acolytes, with Mia in the Cathedral. The monstrous Acolytes are butchering everyone at the wedding, leaving the bride and groom, preparing for the solstice ritual.

"What are they doing?"

"It seems they will use the realm of the dead to escape from our wrath. Use it to hide their position and come back to the mortal plain undetected. We will never find them or their stronghold again," Virgil explains. He snaps his fingers again, showing my body buried under mountains of dirt and mud. "This is you now. Close to death. The closest in your journey."

"Tell me of this crossroad you mentioned."

Virgil waves his hands and an umbilical cord materialises between us. Connecting us. "Our symbiosis is complete, Dante. No more severed ties. No more weakness. Only strength."

The cord vanishes. "I have watched from the shadows of the black matter of your brain. I… no. We are impressed."

A horde of new strangers materialises in front of me. What looks like hundreds. Ranging from an ancient Egyptian warrior, in a red shroud and hood, to a Victorian London looking rogue ruffian in a top hat and leather trench coat.

"Are these… me?"

All the figures speak in unison, "No… We are you."

I look at Virgil. "I don't understand. Why haven't you helped me? With Oizys, or any of it? Why did you let me do the things I did?" I shout in anger.

Virgil hovers closer to me. "A slayer must learn to stand on his own two feet. I'm sorry I pushed you. I needed to prepare you for the harsh reality you will enter. Listen to this story."

My surroundings shift to a tall wooded forest with vibrant green leaves. I can smell the wet grass in my nostrils.

"Where are we?"

Virgil's discombobulated voice speaks to me, "This is the American Frontier, during the British colonisation of the continent, and the persecution of the Native Americans. Watch."

Ahead of me, a group of the indigenous, composed of warriors with bows, or families with children, were fleeing from an unseen assailant. The warriors were gunned down, blood exploding like a Hollywood squib on their bodies.

Not long after, the women and children were taken down too. Falling to the ground, lifeless and deceased.

The gunner came into eye line; it wasn't a British redcoat or coloniser. It was another native. He wore a wolf's pelt over his head and back, creating a hood and cape. He wore nothing else, but the blood of his victims as makeup.

"Oh fuck," I quietly whisper.

"That is Achak. Godslayer of the year 1742 to 1802."

Achak walks to a wounded woman, who didn't die of her bullet wound. She begs for mercy in a language I don't understand. He reveals a tomahawk he had hidden in his cape, and plunges it deep into the woman's skull.

"Why?" I plead.

"Achak was raised in a tribe, as natives were in those days. The Abenaki. They had an eagle who would fly over the tribe every day and drop blue berries from its talons for the people below. The Abenaki believed this eagle was an avatar of Pamola, a spirit that controls the weather. Achak never ate a berry in his time there and was cautious of the bird's intentions. The eagle noticed this. It attacked him when he was a small boy. It picked him up with its talons and flew up a mountain and dropped him off a cliff to die.

"Achak survived, and grew up in the wild. Using his powers and accessing the memories of his predecessors by meditation and rituals, he learnt the truth of his being. He returned home to find his people enslaved by Pamola. Slaves to the weather spirit's command. He returned with weapons and was forced to kill his entire tribe. Men, women and children."

"But why?" I ask back to Virgil. Achak had begun to scalp the warriors at this time.

"Pamola had stripped them of their souls, they were hollow shells of their former selves."

"They didn't look hollow! That poor woman was screaming for her life!"

Just then the scenery dissipates back to black and Virgil appears before me. "Do not fall for their tricks," he spites at me. "Achak learnt that family, connection, must be cast aside in the name of freedom for humanity."

"Do you even care what happens to my wife?"

Virgil pauses. "It is difficult to determine the best course of action with Mia Adler. She has Pandora's blood. She is the only one who can open the cursed box."

"That's why they want to take her and hide, using the other realm. To open Pandora's Box?"

"Yes. It would certainly be better for all, if her bloodline were to cease here and now."

"I can't let her die," I plead my case.

"That is your choice to make. You decide over life and death. Just remember the sacrifice that Achak made. That you made."

I pause and reflect on everything that has transpired. Everything has led to this moment.

"You're offering me the choice to live or die now? I can leave this nightmare behind me?"

"Yes."

"Will it hurt?"

"No. We will let you fade into the hereafter peacefully. No pain. We owe you that much. But think of what you've accomplished. Beating back Herakles. Defying the Acolytes. All your life, you've wanted to be an actor. The art of lying through truth. Pretending to be something else with no direction. You have found what you were meant to be. A warrior."

Silence. "What happens… if I choose to… move on."

"That is a problem for the next slayer."

Those words hit like a jagged knife. I'd only be letting the issue be the next chosen slayer's problem. I could stop them, but Mia is horrified by what I've become. Is it worth living? I could stop them. I can stop them. I will stop them.

I turn and extend my hand towards Virgil with an open palm. Virgil grasps it with a wide smile.

"To tearing shit up?" he remarks.

"To tearing shit up!"

"Good. Let our hatred flow through you. Damn the Gods!"

Our clasped hands begin to light up, and shine.

I open my eyes. My real eyes! I'm surrounded by brown dirt. I begin to push. Strength flowing like nothing I've ever felt before. I claw and dig and scratch my way free. Punching through the final layer of muck. Finally jumping out of my hollow grave with an explosion.

As I breathe out, a hot puff of steam follows like Dragon fire.

My skin is completely grey. My fingertips, now claws. Overhead, thunder claps like a packed football stadium. Lightning echoes and flashes like celebrations. The rain begins to pour like a cyclone.

I raise my head and look skyward and roar. The sky celebrates with a crackle of lightning.

In the distance I see the Cathedral. The black night sky above begins to turn red and spread as far as the eye can see. Even the rain is turning red. The portal to Hell is opening.

Chapter 18

Unholy Matrimony

Despite having a Cathedral, which is located at the top of a small hill with one small road in and out, Guildford is not registered as a city. Instead it is classified as a town.

The council has requested on multiple occasions to have the 'city' certificate granted, but has been rejected a multitude of times.

To combat these rejections, the council, in a surprise one hundred and eighty degrees in attitude, has decided to build bigger, grander buildings. These include high rise buildings and rebuffing the Cathedral with exquisite gargoyles and spindling spires.

So they have put scaffolding up across the entire holy building to pimp it up, with a large yellow crane set up to help with reconstruction.

Tonight on October 31st, Halloween night, It's a bloodbath. What was supposed to be the wedding of a young couple, has become the extermination spot for both families. All in preparation for a ritual, to cross over to the underworld. To escape me.

I begin the long walk up the hill. Thinking back on my adventures the past three days. The train station brawl. Devil's Little Sinners. The chase through London on a stolen bike. Poisoning Herakles. The torture I endured. The horror in the police station. Threatening a grieving mother. Buried alive. All roads have led me here. For one last fight.

Whatever happens. I deserve the outcome, but Mia does not!

Outside the entrance, stood two of the Acolytes. Eris and Momus. Two police cars had been flipped over. The red rain really enhanced the atmosphere to a melancholic tone.

"Well, here I am," my newfound monstrous voice says. I sound like Virgil's tone used to.

The puppet and ghost say nothing. Instead, Momus' body of smoke begins to grow and spiral. Eris chops off his arm and begins to strike sparks over it with two metal pieces, engulfing it in flames. The smoke grows into a massive tornado that spirals the entirety of the Cathedral like a thick barrier. The flames that Eris made combine with the smoke storm, turning into a fiery tornado that encompasses the entire Cathedral

I can just make out the two retreating back inside. They think they can keep me out with something as trivial as a twister.

A ginormous blood whip erupts out of my wrist. I spin it in the air, in the opposite direction of the tornado. My plan is to counter the cyclone's current with my own whip's force.

I wrap the ginormous stream of blood around the twister, and the twister is suffocated by my whip and explodes into tiny crests of ash.

My enemies lie inside.

"Where is she?" I scream as I bust through the large doors to the main hall. Large candles were lit to give a gothic feel to it. Rows of seats with dead people littered across. The bride and groom were at the head of the hall, having their throats slit open by Apate, the blade snake. Brunhilda turned towards me. Bearing her fangs from her wicked leathery face.

"The pup has grown fangs it seems." She raises her arm,

clenching a stone with a rune carved on it. That must be what she tried to hide from me earlier in the hospital. The seven monsters conveyed behind her like a private army. The blood from the couple began to churn and bubble together in a circle. That stone is what controls the Acolytes.

With both whips ignited in a crimson and angry red. I ready my stance for a fight. "I'm not afraid of you. Not anymore."

"Is that so?" Brunhilda spits.

"You're the one who's planning to run away."

She screams. The rune stone flashes blue The Acolytes all charge at once toward me like a pack of wolves. Brunhilda tends to the birthing portal.

They all strike the ground where I stood at once, but I was too quick and leaped overhead, flinging the whips down and slicing at them where they now stood. They all jumped away, except for Oizys, who was cut in half. Her barbed wire the only thing keeping her top and bottom halves connected.

Nemesis was quick too. He sprang toward me in mid-air and slashed at my ribs with his scaly hands. I blocked, but the force hit me back down to ground floor.

Nemesis springs from the ceiling back toward me with his large jaws open for a chomp. My reactions were quicker, I grab his jaws and twist them as he gets close enough, a large crack proves I broke his jaws.

"You mudarfufer!" he tries to say.

I then kick him in the eye, popping it clean out of its socket. It bounces along the floor like a ping pong ball. Two down. Five to go.

Geras shows her face next, still clutching her dead bouquet.

"I know you don't want to do this," I reason with her, hoping to get through to the Esta persona.

"She won't let me go. No one will." She fires her flower needles at me. Some puncture through to my skin, but they barely hurt now. I just brush them off. Geras kneels down, as if ready to die, for her nightmare to end. I begin to pace forward, but a large sword pierces through the back of my shoulder and lifts me up.

Apate spins me around so he can look me in the eye. Face to rotting face.

"Always got to keep an eye open aye?" Apate mocks me. "Never turn your back on an opponent."

Apate's arrogance will cost him. He brought me in close enough to rip his head from his spine. Which I did. The knife covered body drops down. The head keeps talking.

"Put me back!" But I just kick it away like a football.

Geras sneaks up right behind me, sucks in air and howls it out. The force flings me through a window and I land back outside on top of a parked car. Ouch.

I slouch off of the bent car roof and get my bearings. Suddenly Eris the puppet returns with four of the wedding guests now zombified as his slaves, just like the exhibits back at the museum. The zombies were slow and easy to hit back. Eris darted in to get a cheap hit once in a while, but it was no issue. I sling a whip onto Eris and the friction causes his wooden body to burst into orange flame. I even think I could hear him moan in pain as he fell. Even the rain could not quell the fire. The invisible strings used on the poor people snapped as well, as they too fell limp. Four down. Three to go.

I rush back inside. The portal to the realm of the dead was now brimming with life. It was almost open. Geras floundered about, waiting for me to make the first move, but I fet a chill in the air, almost like smoke…

I quickly U-turn and wrap my whips around Momus like an

Octopus grabbing its prey. He can't phase through the blood streams, he's stuck. His body also becomes more solid and less gaseous. Becoming a naked bald blue man, choking, as his body begins metamorphoses.

Before Geras could even flinch. I lasso her and pull her toward me like Indiana Jones with one of his damsels, but unlike him, I stick my fist through her heart.

"I'm sorry, Esta."

"They… won't… let me… go." She disintegrates.

Now only Moros remains.

"Dante!" That voice. Mia!

I look up to find Brunhilda flapping her ugly wings with my wife in her clutches.

"You won't win!" the warrior angel screeches. She busts a hole in the ceiling and flies out. I don't care where the spider is, I have to save my wife.

The roof of the Cathedral was covered in metal bars and scaffolding. Wooden panels rocked in the wind. Brunhilda stood at the other end, next to the tower that housed the giant bell.

"How does it feel to be a monster?" she crows over the wind.

"Says the Hollywood movie star."

"You, boy! Should learn some respect. Your eyes are as red as any demon in the pits of hell!"

"Are we going to end this or what?"

Brunhilda throws Mia aside. Raises her arms for battle.

Splooch! Click! Click! Click!

Moros thrusts his arm through Brunhilda's throat and decapitates her. Her lifeless body drops down through the hole in the roof and plummets down into the mouth to the dead realm. The controlling rune stone was dropped next to the spider in the panic. Moros picks it up, and breaks it in his hands, reducing it to mere pebbles and fragments that get scattered in the wind, never to be seen again.

He looks at me with his sad eyes and chants, "Charon!"

Inky tendrils spurt out of his body. Six to be exact and all fire off in different directions. They soon come back, holding the bodies of the defeated Acolytes like ragdolls.

"You're in for it now, fucker!" the head of Apate mocks as it flies past me.

The seven bodies join into one. Moulding and churning. Cracking and weaving. A large hand pops out, followed by another, and two large legs. It stood upright.

It looked like a demon made of charred black wood. It stood about fifteen metres high. Two long splintering logs for horns and large sticks spurting out of its back like a porcupine. The eyes were red with black pupils. The cracks between its wooden plating glowed orange and squirted the black ink substance out. This was Charon. The Ferryman of the dead. It all made sense. The Acolytes were leaking water from the river Styx. That's what the black substance was.

"Oh it's good to be back," he chimed like an opera singer. "That smell?" He sniffs the air and pinpoints Mia. "Ah, Pandora's blood. You're who we're after. You'd make a grand Acolyte."

"Leave her alone!" I shout.

"Godslayer." Charon places Mia at the top of the bell tower. "You're the nuisance I must deal with. Hmm?"

I'm surprised the roof can support the giant's weight. "It's just you and me."

"No, boy! You face seven!" The seven Acolyte faces pop out of his chest and scream like a jump scare from a horror movie.

I rush toward the wooden monster and hook a tether from

my whip onto the huge crane and boost up to the metal frame of the fixed tower. I hit hard with a loud *clang* ringing in my ears.

"Oh no you don't!" Charon claps the crane and begins to climb after me. "The fun has only just begun!"

I scurry quickly to the driver's cab, but quickly dart up the load jib, all the way to where the hook is anchored, to further our distance still. Charon stops at where the cabin is.

"Have a nice ride!" Charon slices the jib of the crane with his razor bark fingers.

I hold on tight as the jib comes crashing down back on top of the Cathedral roof.

Bang!

I roll away from the carnage, unscathed, miraculously.

Charon plummets back down, in front of me. "Nowhere to hide!"

I rush over towards him, and slide under him as he tries to claw and slash at me. I anchor a whip to the top of the high tower and swing up to the peak. He's too strong for me to take on. I land next to Mia with a superhero landing like fashion.

"I'm so sorry for everything, Mia."

"It's okay. Just save us."

Charon swings his arm at the tower structure, destroying its supporting bricks like it was swatting flies, it begins to slant like the leaning Tower of Pisa.

The bricks snap, crackle and burst under the pressure. Charon swings his arms around and begins to pull. The tower pivots and sways, before finally falling, the bell singing the blues as the tower falls. I hold Mia tight.

The tower crashes into the roof, obliterating it and crashing down to the ground floor like a meteorite. I accidentally let Mia slip through my grip. She falls, and is trying to reach for me. Time seems to slow and then stop around me. My only focus being on her. I spring forth, reaching for her, but Charon whips me aside and laughs.

"No!" I shout.

She slips through my eye line. I can't see her. Fading into the dust below.

"Even you are powerless against the unstoppable tide of death!" Charon says.

I failed. I failed her.

Charon throws me into the rubble below. The once famous landmark now a battleground of titanic proportions with the red rain falling through the massive open skyline above us. I don't feel the will to keep fighting. The portal bursts into life. It's fully open.

"Ooo. A portal home. Pandora's heir will love to join my little family and feel welcomed in our home." Charon picks through the rubble looking for my wife.

"Ahhhh!" Charon shrieks in pain all of a sudden and is hit in the head, knocking him over. Who saved me?

"Hello, Dante." Herakles steps forth, triumphant. No longer bestial looking. No longer golden. He looked like a regular strong man. He helped me to my feet.

"I thought you were dead?"

"My death was greatly exaggerated, oh, and here." He steps to the side, revealing a very much alive Mia. "I got here in the nick of time."

I embrace Mia and she reciprocates the affection. "I'm so sorry! I'm so sorry!"

Mia rests her palms on my cheek. "I know. You know, I know."

I then face my former foe. "Thank you."

"Well, perhaps… I can redeem my family… by saving yours." We both smile. A newfound respect forged between us.

"How touching!" Charon rises. Angry. "Enemies to friends. How cliché."

Herakles charges and wrestles Charon to the floor by grabbing his ankles and heaving.

"Mia, do you still have the speaker?" I quickly ask and grab her shoulders to enhance the urgency of the situation.

She rummages through her pockets and pulls out the branded bomb. "What are you going to do?"

"Something I hoped I wouldn't have to. He's too strong." I then rush to join the fight. "Herakles! Push him into that portal in the ground!"

"I'll try!" he shouts back and begins to push Charon, but the Ferryman gets back to his knees, and kicks Herakles like a pro footballer at the Premier League final.

Herakles flies into the exposed giant bell amongst the rubble. A metallic *gong,* to signify the impact.

Charon hovers over me and crushes me with his giant trunk of a foot. Flattening me like a pancake. "It's over!" he proclaims. He raises his foot to stomp again…

"Wait!" Mia gets between the foot and myself like a human shield. Charon stops his movement, motionless as a statue.

"Why?"

"If you let him live… I'll join your family."

Charon kneels down to Mia's mere mortal level. Strokes his bark covered chin. "Deal," he finalises.

"Just let me say goodbye."

"Fine. Make it quick."

Mia comes down to my face, and kisses me on the lips. "You are the man I married, never forget that. I love you."

Charon grabs Mia and begins to stride to the portal.

I feel like I'm having an out of body experience. I see my brutalised body amongst the rubble, but I begin to smile. Ecstatic at Mia's proclamation of love.

My skin turns back to a healthy colour, no longer grey and with a touch of vampirism. My claw tips return to freshly cut fingernails. The darkening around my eyes ceases to exist, and my eye colour turns back to an ocean pearl blue.

It's like all the hate inside me, has been replaced with love.

I stand. Powerful. With newfound purpose. I ignite my whips, but the stream colour has changed. Instead of a bloody red, they are a bright white, like they've been healed and ceased to bleed.

The speaker bomb is still intact. I grab it.

"Hey!"

Charon sighs and turns around. "Don't you know when to give up?"

I slash a whip at the beast's ankles, cleaving them both off like a guillotine cut. He lets go of Mia in confusion. I jump forward and catch her. Redeeming myself for my past miss.

"Herakles! Now would be a god time for a tag out!"

The redeemed hero of Sparta frees himself from being trapped under debris. He grasps the massive bell and flings himself like a spring at Charon's face, striking him hard with the ringing, thick metal.

Gong!

The force of the impact knocks off the coarse wooden plating on the left of his face, revealing a horrid skull of alien proportions.

The wooden creature falls back in a howl of distress, down into the portal, but he grabs the edge of the rim of the portal as he falls. Clinging on.

I jump down into the hellhole, land on his face and jam the bomb in its now hollow eye. It begins to beep. Counting down to detonation. I can see down into this dark damned dimension. It's indescribable. A hellhole by all accounts and merit.

"Nooooo!" Charon screams. His plans snuffed like a small, weak candle.

"Dante!" Mia calls for me.

I give her one last look, with a façade of fake confidence stricken across my face.

Flash. Silence. Nothing.

Chapter 19

I am Dante… Godslayer

"DANTE!" the sinister voice wakes me again.

Wait… I've done this already. Déjà vu. I'm in my bed. How did I get here? I just blew up the realm of the dead. I should be dead! Charon!

I look around, even check under the sheets, but the only unholy thing here is my smell.

Checking my phone reveals the most perplexing puzzle. The date shows October 29th.

I rush down the stairs, forgetting to put on any clothes, seeing Mia in the living room on our brown leather sofa.

"Hello… handsome," she says uncomfortably upon seeing me stark naked.

"Are you okay?" I ask.

"Yeah, why wouldn't I be?"

"What about Charon? Or Herakles?"

"Who?"

I pause for a moment before my next question… "Have we been to Devil's Little Sinners?"

"No that's tonight."

Oh my god. I'm in the past! I throw up on our nice carpet.

That night. Mia goes out to London by herself. I ask to stay behind, saying I feel unwell, but want her to have a good time.

We hug goodbye, and she leaves to take a taxi to the station.

I walk into the bathroom, and look at my reflection. "Virgil?"

"Yes, Dante?" My reflection shifts to look like Virgil's damaged and scarred state.

"Oh thank God. What the hell is going on?"

"I have a few theories, but nothing concrete."

"So what now? Did everything we do not matter?"

"I don't know. Just remember this…"

"What?"

"Reality… is not always a linear path that is trodden."

Later in the evening. I'm sitting in my favourite chair in the living room. Contemplating what to do next. Mia does not remember anything. It's like she's another person to me now. She doesn't know who she is. Who's after her.

And what about Herakles? Is he still my friend now? Or will he revert to his former self now? The Covenant is still out there. Brunhilda may still be alive and who else is in this group?

Clover must still have eyes on me. They knew who I was after all.

But now, the public doesn't know about me. My secret is a secret again.

I have to go. I know that.

Sitting at the kitchen table, a nice hot cup of tea next to me and my last few couple of chocolate biscuits, I begin to write Mia a letter:

Dear Mia,

You deserve better than this, but to spare you any more pain, I have to leave in this manner. There are things that I must do, to protect you. I know it's unreasonable to not give a reason, but it's the only way to keep you safe.

I've seen things that no man should ever have to, endured what no one ever should, and these things have caught up to me.

Know that I always love you, and will watch out for you always.

I hope to return home soon.

Love, always, Dante.

I seal the letter in an envelope and leave it on the kitchen table.

I pack a backpack full of essentials, water, food, money, a toothbrush and a sleeping bag, but leave credit cards and my phone behind.

I open the garage. My father's bike stands. Untampered and no longer a broken slab of parts.

I have a second chance now, to do better. Be better. Fight with love. Not through hate.

The bike revs to life as I turn the ignition on, and I leave my home. Without looking back.

My first stop is the Guildford Royal Surrey Hospital. I'm looking for Doctor Wells, and her secret lab.

"Excuse me," I ask reception. "Doctor Wells?"

"She's on break at the moment," the receptionist replies.

"Tell her it's Dante Adler, and that I know about Sekhmet. She'll know what that means."

The receptionist complies, but gives a slight shrug with her eyes and goes to tell Wells in the break room nearby. She comes back.

"She said to come immediately," she says with confusion.

Doctor Wells was standing nervously, leaving her half-eaten chicken and cucumber sandwich on the table next to her cappuccino. "Dante!" she exasperates.

I stick my palm out, signifying there is no need to explain.

"Why don't we talk in your secret lab instead?"

Wells takes my hand, closes the break room door and mutters a chant under her breath. She ends it with a rhythmic knock on the door. She opens it, revealing we have somehow teleported to the secret dream therapy lab.

She takes me to her office. The same one from before. Or is it technically later? Time travel can be so confusing.

"First things first," I begin. "I'll take that beats speaker that you designed for Clover to blow up a dimension. It's currently in your desk drawer."

Grey Wells slowly takes out the speaker and hands me the device. I open the back of it and remove the battery. Powering the device down, and finally snap it in two.

Wells jumps, believing it was about to explode. "Things don't work without a battery," I light-heartedly comment.

"How do you know?" she asks me.

I tell her my story. The Acolytes and Brunhilda with her secret Covenant. My powers. The Hallowed Solstice. Mia's true lineage. The fact I know she is Sekhmet and is trying to clone her son that I killed in a past life. How Clover are using her for her technological prowess for their own misguided purposes. And finally about being sent back in time after detonating the bomb in Charon's fat stupid face.

"Wow." Is all she could say.

"I'm trying to do better now. With this second chance. When I was last here. I did something horrible. I won't ever resort to that level again. But you need to stop these experiments on these poor people. For me."

"Okay," she firmly says, like she plans to honour my request. "What will you do now?"

"Firstly, make sure no portals to other dimensions are

opened in two days."

"Where is Mia, by the way?"

I breath heavily. "Do me a favour, Doc. Don't tell her you saw me." I stand and begin to walk away. "And you don't have to hide under Clover's blouse any more. I'll protect you from them and your family." With those words I make my exit, and leave Wells to contemplate my most generous offer.

Forty-eight hours later, on Halloween night. I watch the wedding take place in the Cathedral from a safe distance in the trees. No monsters intervened. No magic portals to another realm.

I recovered the blood whips. Had to break into the Museum again. Barry was still alive, but he didn't see me. The whips were still white instead of red, so at least that is still the same. But what about the realm of the dead? At what cost have I gained this victory?

"You have been very busy," a high-pitched voice cackles from the dark.

"Show yourself!" I call out.

A brown horse trots out of the dark. Strange, but I don't give it a second thought. The mare then opens its mouth, revealing rows of shark teeth and begins to cough something up. A bloody hand and arm reach out, followed by a completely naked small pale man. The stallion then erupts in sharp flames, but quickly extinguishes and snuffs out, in a blink and you'll miss it fashion.

A thin man in a purple medieval jester's outfit comes out of the shadows. He had pointed cheekbones and facial features like his brow and nose. His lips were black. His arms and legs looked too thin and malnourished to support even his hollow body. He picks up the small naked man and shrinks him to the size of a steak, and all of a sudden eats it.

“Sorry about that,” the voice continues. “I do love a grand entrance, and I was a bit peckish.”

“Who are you?”

The Jester bows, after finishing his disturbing snack. The small bells on his hat rattling. “I am Loki. God of Mischief. It is an honour to meet you.”

“And brother of Thor,” I add.

“My most famous accomplishment, and also total bullshit. I share no relation to that fat red-haired oath. He’s a blunt object. Brutal. No precision in swinging that almighty hammer of his. I’m of a much finer craft, like a sewing needle. And you, by the way, and more importantly, are Dante Adler. Godslayer.”

I nod. The jester jumps up and down with excitement. “What do you want?” I ask it.

“Oh, Dante. You have accomplished so much. We Gods have sensed the disturbance in the timeline. Blowing up the realm of the dead? What compelled you to do that?”

“Love, dipshit. You planning to somehow undo it?”

“Oh, on the contrary. We have decided to let this little transgression slide.”

“That’s thoughtful,” I say sarcastically.

“When that bomb went off. It rippled across time and space. You didn’t blow up the realm of the dead. You divided it. Broke it into tiny pieces. Why do you think different religions have different versions of the Underworld or Hell? The Gods all want their own retrospective afterlife to govern. And we can’t forget about poor Charon, forever divided into seven, breaking his memories and doomed to repeat the time loop of being killed by you. The blow as well sent you back through time. Cool right? It’s so weird.” Loki breathes heavily and gives me a faraway look. He scoops a pile of dirt in his palm and lets it slide through his fingers like sand in an hour glass.

"Time… Reality… They were never weaved in a straight line. It's tangled… Looped… Infinite."

Loki is as cryptic as an enigma code.

So, anyway, I created different forms of the afterlife? Neat. And I'm the reason Charon needs seven avatars, because I divided him too? Cool. Being sent back through time, still feels surreal to hear. "So why are you here?"

Loki flips a dry bloodstained silver bullet into my hand. "You have a debt to pay me, and I'm calling up the tab."

I tense the muscles in my fist. Clenching them so tightly, I dig into my nails, drawing blood forth. My story has evidently only just begun.

Epilogue

Another Perspective. From Another Time

The Godslayer has vanquished the Acolytes. Banished Charon back to the past. Been given a second chance for his life choices. Angered the narrow-minded Gods, from their up on high White City, perched in the clouds. He is doing very well for such a novice.

But now, the destined bullet has been delivered. His debt must be repaid.

The coming storm of events rumbles louder. I can feel it.

Pandora's blood will be spilled.

The King of monsters will rise again.

The Sin Harbinger will follow like a plague.

No eyes can unsee these coming calamities.

The Dark God's grand design weaves itself again. Spindling on the fracturing wheel of time.

The isolation of all, is on its way.

Maybe this time it will be different. But I won't hold my breath. I'll be watching you… Dante.